BOOK 3
IN THE
OPERATION:
MIDDLE OF THE
GARDEN SERIES

OF CONSUMING FIRE

Micah Persell

AUTHOR OF *OF ETERNAL LIFE, OF THE KNOWLEDGE OF GOOD AND EVIL,* AND *EMMA: THE WILD AND WANTON EDITION*

CRIMSON ROMANCE
F+W Media, Inc.

This edition published by
Crimson Romance
an imprint of F+W Media, Inc.
10151 Carver Road, Suite 200
Blue Ash, Ohio 45242
www.crimsonromance.com

ISBN 10: 1-4405-7032-9
ISBN 13: 978-1-4405-7032-2
eISBN 10: 1-4405-7033-7
eISBN 13: 978-1-4405-7033-9

For Forest—
An amazing man and top-shelf friend

Acknowledgments

As always, a wellspring of gratitude goes to my first readers. Christine, Tiffany, Joyce, and Nathan—I couldn't have done this without you.

Glossary of Terms

Compulsion: A phenomenon specific to angels. Once an angel plans out his or her mission, free will is not a possibility. At a certain point, the Compulsion will take over. The angel will complete the mission regardless of whether he or she wants to.

Daughters and Sons of Men: Humans.

Fall, the: A heavenly being who succumbs to his or her Temptation, Falls: a phenomenon through which the heavenly being loses divine status and some or all of his or her powers.

Impulse Pair: Anyone who eats of the Tree of Eternal Life will experience the Impulse—a phenomenon in which the human pairs with his or her intended mate. The humans in an Impulse pair will experience intense longing to be with their Impulse mate, and the longer they abstain from each other, the more intense the side effects of the Impulse. Impulse pain will grow until it become debilitating. Impulse pain can only be cured and avoided by the Impulse pair's consummation.

Knowledge, the: The ability, provided by the Tree of the Knowledge of Good and Evil, to determine upon touch whether someone's intentions are *good* or *evil*.

Sons of God: Angels; not always "sons," which is an archaic reference used to encompass all of a species. Angels can also be female.

Temptation: Each heavenly being will at some point encounter his or her Temptation—the one thing that will tempt them to

Fall. Temptations can take several forms, but the most common is a daughter (or son) of man.

Tree of Eternal Life: The tree in the Garden of Eden that bears fruit that turns living beings immortal.

Tree of the Knowledge of Good and Evil: The tree in the Garden of Eden that caused the Fall of mankind. The fruit of this tree counteracts some of the effects of the Tree of Eternal Life. The fruit gifts humans with the Knowledge.

Voice, the: A mysterious, disembodied entity that speaks directly to the minds of those who have eaten of the Tree of Eternal Life.

Epigraph

The Lord God made all kinds of trees grow out of the ground—trees that were pleasing to the eye and good for food. In the middle of the garden were the tree of life and the tree of the knowledge of good and evil.

Genesis 2:9-10

After he drove the man out, he placed on the east side of the Garden of Eden cherubim and a flaming sword flashing back and forth to guard the way to the tree of life.

Genesis 3:24

Now it came about, when men began to multiply on the face of the land, and daughters were born to them, that the sons of God saw that the daughters of men were beautiful; and they took wives for themselves...

Genesis 6:1-2

Chapter One

Dr. Grace Tucker pulled herself deeper into the corner and tucked her arms tighter around her unshapely belly. As her hands and arms touched her large middle, it repulsed her nearly as much as it seemed to repulse the opposite sex. No, there was no disappearing a plus-sized woman, but her sloppy appearance got most people to look away quickly, which was as close as Grace was ever going to get to being blessedly invisible.

And, not for the first time, she desperately wished to be invisible.

Grace huddled in the main room of the top-secret government facility where the Trees stood. As always, she ignored them. She was never awed by the ancient trees. She'd taken one cursory glance at their branches that most described as majestic. Their fruit—covered in glittering diamonds for the Tree of Eternal Life, swirling black and white for the Tree of the Knowledge of Good and Evil—was interesting only in that it loosely related to her work. She didn't stand there and stare at them for hours as she was told was the expected behavior for new employees.

And yet right now, Grace wasn't the only one ignoring the Trees. The somber mood in the facility was nearly suffocating. Not one of the dozens of employees had spoken in hours. They moped from room to room, desk to desk, casting great, wide-eyed glances upon everyone they crossed. But that wasn't the reason Grace retreated to the corner.

They were *touching* one another.

Any person they came into reaching distance with. A hand on the shoulder. A hug. A squeeze of the arm or lingering pat on the back.

It was only a matter of time before one of them tried to touch *her*. And that simply was not going to work. End of story.

And, so, she was in the closest thing to a corner the domed room provided.

A young soldier in army fatigues walked by, and Grace went rigid, holding her breath until he passed.

He didn't once glance in her direction. Grace's breath flew from her frozen lungs even as her heart seized at the casual snub. She hugged herself tighter as she cursed her weak emotions. Without fail, every time her carefully cultivated armor of acerbic wit and slovenly appearance actually worked as she'd meant it to by keeping others away, her irrational side would come up bruised, as though it didn't know perfectly well the reasons human contact was not in Grace's cards.

She sighed almost silently, and forced herself to look cheerfully upon the fact that standing in the corner was working. She would make it through this. She *would*. It wouldn't be like all of the other times. There would be no scene. No gut-wrenching screams shooting from her body without her control. No hysterical sobs. No sedation. No awkward return to work. No inevitable summons to the boss. No starting over with the knowledge that this was her life—on repeat.

She closed her eyes. The sad truth was, this *was* her life. And right now, she was huddled in the corner, praying to be invisible, worrying with all of her strength that someone would touch her.

But her friend's impending death? Not even a blip on her emotional radar. Jericho Edwards was dying, and Grace was worried about herself.

Jericho was everyone's favorite, but for a reason Grace couldn't explain, he was *her* favorite as well. It had been thirteen long years since Grace considered a man as anything other than something to be avoided at all costs. Thirteen years since Grace had carefully erected a wall around her heart. And yet, somehow, Jericho found his way around that wall the tiniest bit.

It might have been the very obvious fact that Jericho would never, ever pose a threat to her. She'd known two seconds after being introduced to him that he was head over heels in love with someone: his Impulse mate, Dahlia. Jericho was nice to *everyone*, men and women alike. In fact, Grace had never met anyone so good.

And he'd taken one look at her—her frumpy clothes, excess body weight, bird's nest of red hair, black-rimmed glasses, and man-hating glare—and deemed her a friend, working tirelessly at cultivating a relationship with her when everyone else just avoided her.

And now, he was dying. Worse, his survival depended upon *Grace* and Grace's work.

Three months and a week or so ago, Jericho cut his finger on the sword—the artifact that Grace was commissioned to work on. It was a flesh wound that should have healed in seconds given that Jericho, Dahlia, Eli, and Abilene were all immortal after eating the fruit from the Tree of Eternal Life. But the simple wound hadn't healed. And things came to a head a few days ago when Jericho returned to the facility with his brand new wife, Dahlia. In the process of moving, Jericho managed to rip the tiny, unhealed wound wide open from the tip of his finger into his palm. It had been bleeding profusely ever since, and his body couldn't keep up.

And suddenly, Dr. Grace Tucker was very much in demand. She couldn't count the number of times she had to remind them "I'm not that kind of doctor." Their situation was so unique that her PhD in dead languages made her much more qualified to help Jericho than an MD would on its best day, but her work took more time than medication or surgery ever would.

She'd made her breakthrough this morning.

The ancient, dead language on the sword said *What the Tree gives, the Sword takes. What the Sword takes, the Tree gives.*

At least, she was ninety-nine percent sure that's what it said.

Grace gritted her teeth, closed her eyes, and reassured herself that she was never wrong when it came to her work. Never. She was wrong when it came to everything else, but her work was infallible.

That's why she was here. She was the single most prestigious language expert in the world. And it was going to change her life. That was the plan. She'd worked hard to make sure no one noticed her. The weight she'd gained, the fashion-backward wardrobe, the overt hostility—when she couldn't disappear into her surroundings, she kept people away with every weapon her extensive intelligence and vast vocabulary could come up with.

But Grace's secret dream *was* recognition. She just wanted it on her terms. She was going to make *the* discovery of all time with this sword. It was the work she'd been waiting for her entire career. And now it was here. And, as long as her translation was right, it was about to save one of only four immortal human beings on the planet.

Career. Made.

Everyone would know her name; everyone would know she was something. And the best part? She'd be absolutely untouchable in a way she could not dream of cultivating on her own. No one walked up to the winner of the Nobel Prize and gave them a hug. They got the recognition without all the messy social baggage associated with being members of the human race. They were members of a class considered above such things. And Grace couldn't wait to be admitted into their ranks.

Grace's eyes snapped open when she heard the sharp clack of men's shoes on the hard floor of the facility. Sergeant Collins was approaching.

Grace shrank back further into her corner, her shoulders bending in on themselves, but it was too late: he was looking right at her, and double damn, he'd noticed she was trying to turn into wallpaper if the arch of one of his salt and pepper eyebrows was any indication.

He stopped before her, and Grace couldn't prevent the hitch in her breathing. Reaching distance. The man was within reaching distance. She bit her bottom lip to avoid a whimper.

"Dr. Tucker?" Sergeant Collins asked in his smooth, Southern whisky drawl. He then looked her over once more. His eyes softened. He took a step back and crossed his arms behind him, effecting "at ease" posture.

Relief flooded through her so strongly it momentarily overshadowed the embarrassment she felt at having someone else recognize her reticence at human contact. But only momentarily. Damn it, why couldn't she be normal?

She straightened to her full height—a whole five feet five inches—and worked her hardest to look as un-crazy as possible. "What can I do for you, sir?" A lock of her frizzy, red hair fell over her glasses, blocking Sergeant Collins from sight. She shoved it out of the way, tucking it behind one of the pencils stuffed into her "style" of the day.

"Nothing more than you've done, ma'am," he said with polite distance. "I've come to report that your findings seem to be accurate."

Grace wanted to sag in relief, but was so wary of causing Sergeant Collins to think any less of her that she clenched her jaw and forced iron into her spine. No one would know how worried she'd been about her translation. She'd emit cool confidence all day long. Her "findings" included the recommendation that whatever damage the sword caused could be un-done by administering the fruit of the Tree of Eternal Life topically. They'd been forcing the fruit down Jericho's throat for days to no effect. It was a nuance of the language that had given Grace the idea to apply the fruit to the site of Jericho's wound.

"So, Jericho's recovering?" Grace forced herself to ask, alarmed a little at the obvious worry in her voice. She didn't care about him that much, did she?

A new voice sounded as it approached. "His skin is knitting together before our eyes." Dahlia Edward's brown eyes peeked around Collins's shoulder, warm for the first time ever that Grace witnessed.

Grace actually liked Dahlia a lot, and not just because Jericho did. Grace hadn't met many people who seemed to hate all others as much as Dahlia did. She was even more socially hostile than Grace. It was…refreshing.

"They think he'll wake up any moment now, and I want to be there when he does, but I had to come thank you first," Dahlia continued.

Grace felt her eyes widen. "Thanks" often involved touch of some kind. "That's not necessary," Grace muttered, crowding the corner again.

Dahlia rolled her eyes. "Relax, Red," she said with a laugh. "God, it's not like we're going to attack you with hugs or anything."

Grace didn't laugh. She didn't even notice when the two before her exchanged a worried look as her eyes glazed, and her mind turned over one of Dahlia's words.

Attack. Attack. Attack.

A loud snap erupted in front of her face.

Grace refocused to see Dahlia's fingers before her eyes as the woman snapped again, this time accompanied by a sharp, "Grace!"

Grace sucked in a breath.

"Is she…" Sergeant Collins trailed off as both women's heads snapped around to glare at him.

Grace opened her mouth to speak, but was cut off with Dahlia's curt, "She's fine, Collins, God." She then stood directly in front of Grace, blocking her from Collins's sight, giving her a chance to compose herself. "Nothing some lunch and a good night's sleep won't fix. We've run her ragged. Give her some *grace*." Dahlia snorted.

Collins threw Dahlia a wobbly smile. "I'll just…um…call Miss Esperanza then. Tell her Jericho's fine." His mouth moved like a caress over the name of Dahlia's former mother-in-law, his accent adding at least two syllables, and his eyes twinkling like a kid.

Dahlia looked at Grace and winked. "You do that, Collins."

He cast one more concerned look toward Grace's corner, not quite meeting her eyes, and backed off, hurrying away to his office.

As Dahlia watched him go, her hand fell to the small bump beneath her shirt. Grace was pretty sure she was the only person in the facility who had guessed that Jericho and Dahlia were expecting. There had been no announcement; there hadn't been time before Jericho fell gravely ill. But Dahlia made that little movement often when she thought no one was looking.

She turned to Grace now and arched a perfect eyebrow.

"I really am fine," Grace offered weakly.

Dahlia scoffed and muttered something in Spanish that Grace perfectly understood—dead languages weren't her only specialty. Grace bristled. "Look, I'll just get back to work." The news of Jericho's recovery was already spreading if the increased chatter in the room was any indication. She could re-join life now. She needed to get started on writing this up, though she knew publishing any of her top-secret findings was going to be an uphill battle. Possibly an impossible one.

Dahlia nodded once and began to turn away.

"Hey," Grace blurted. Dahlia turned back to her. "Um…when he wakes up. Tell Jericho…I'm glad he's okay." Grace was shocked to find out she meant it.

Dahlia's eyes roved Grace's face for a moment, but then she smiled. "You've got it, Red." She took two steps toward the medical wing, then stopped.

Grace watched the black waves cascading down Dahlia's back rustle as the stunning Latina tilted her head to the side.

"Do you hear that?" Dahlia asked.

Grace frowned. "Hear what?"

Just then, the lights flickered. A distant rumbling seemed to seep in through the walls of the facility.

All of the hopeful chatter in the room faded and then fizzled out as people began to look around curiously.

A huge clap of thunder rent through the building with such force that loose items throughout the main room clattered where they sat.

The lights went out completely.

Emergency lights along the walls illuminated, casting Dahlia's caramel skin in an unearthly glow as Grace stared at her in barely subdued panic. The others in the room began to mumble to each other, their voices rising in pitch. She felt her nails digging into the skin of her arms and realized she was hugging herself again.

A man in a lab coat raced into the main room, skidding around the door and barreling toward Dahlia as soon as he spotted her. "He's waking!" he yelled at Jericho's wife. "Come quickly."

Dahlia took a quick step toward him, but then stumbled. She threw out an arm to catch herself against the wall. "*Shit*," Grace heard her mutter.

Dahlia spun around and pinned Grace with a wide-eyed look. "Earthquake," she told Grace in an odd, disbelieving tone. "Big one."

Dahlia lunged forward and grabbed Grace by the arm, hauling her quickly to a nearby desk and shoving herself and Grace in the small area beneath it.

Shooting pains emanated from the skin Dahlia's fingers touched. Grace hissed and tried to wrench her arm from Dahlia's grip as she spluttered, "What—how do you—"

"I can hear it coming," she said impatiently. "Take cover!" she bellowed to all the gawkers.

No sooner had the words left her mouth than the first wave hit the building. A sound, louder than the eardrum-cracking clap of thunder, ricocheted through the room like a freight train, and Grace watched with wide eyes as the floor began to ripple at the edge of the room and move toward them like oncoming ocean waves.

And, even though paralyzed with fear, all Grace could think of was the scorching pain of Dahlia's fingers where they still clutched her arm.

Screams began to echo as the men and women who worked at the facility realized what was happening. Feet thundered as everyone sought shelter.

But Grace scrambled away from Dahlia and out into the open as soon as the woman's grip on Grace's arm slackened.

Dahlia's arm snaked out and captured the back of Grace's jacket. "What the *hell*?"

"Don't *touch me*!" Grace shrieked so loudly that Dahlia drew back in shock.

A huge chunk of plaster fell from the ceiling to land right beside Grace. A cloud of white exploded from its impact and dusted both of them. Desks began to skitter across the floor.

"Do you want to die?" Dahlia yelled, blinking the white powder from her lashes.

Die or be touched? No contest. Grace didn't move.

The earthquake gained in intensity. The glass that made up the ceiling of the dome tinkled and Grace looked up as a crack spider-webbed from one end of the dome to the other.

"Okay," Dahlia said fast and low. "I won't touch you. Just get your ass under here right now!"

Grace dragged her eyes from the ceiling to look into the dim space beneath the desk. Dahlia pressed herself against the side, leaving more than enough room for Grace to fit without having to be against the other woman. And still she hesitated.

Across the dome, bookshelves began to fall like dominoes, each one hitting the ground with a resounding boom. The tinkling of the glass ceiling increased and one or two shards escaped and plummeted toward the ground.

With a deep breath for courage, Grace dove into the area beside Dahlia just as the ceiling gave way.

The glass chimed like clock-tower bells as it fell. It tinkled off of every surface and bounced from the floor in glittering arcs. Grace watched in horror as a huge shard caught one of the soldiers as he tried to dive under a desk a few feet away. His scream cut off as the glass sliced through his chest and pinned him to the floor right where Grace had been kneeling seconds before.

Grace huddled into the corner and buried her face against the wood of the desk so hard she thought her nose might break.

The waves of the ground moved as though alive beneath Grace, hitting her in the shins and knees again and again as she knelt and causing her stomach to lurch as though seasick. Beside her, she heard Dahlia begin to recite the rosary in Spanish in a low, breathless voice. As a backdrop, the glass on the floor clacked and pinged as the entire building shimmied with the rage of the earth.

And in the next heartbeat, everything stopped.

Grace's frantic breaths in the sudden absence of sound were excruciatingly loud, but the silence didn't last for long. Moans from the wounded began to fill the air.

She heard her boss, Eli Johnson, bellowing his past-due pregnant wife's name as he barreled through the dome from his office and toward the medical wing.

"Jericho," Dahlia breathed next to her. Then she scrambled from her hiding spot, sliding in the blood that slicked across the floor from the impaled man before gaining purchase and sprinting in Eli's wake.

Grace stared dumbfounded at the glassy eyes of the dead man in front of her before forcing herself to emerge from the desk.

Utter destruction waited for her. Her eyes skimmed over the demolished main room of the facility. Everything was…gone. Desks were smashed. Books were flung to every wall of the room. The glass on the floor glittered like diamonds among the pools of blood. It looked like after-pictures of a tornado.

But the trees stood resolute in the center of the room. Not one fruit had fallen from their branches. And on the desk beneath them, where Grace did her work, the sword glowed. The sword, usually covered with flickering green and gold flames, was now… *angry.* It was the only word she could use to describe what she was seeing. The green and gold flames had morphed into red and black. The metal, engraved with the words she had translated to say *what the tree gives, the sword takes; what the sword takes, the tree gives* was now pulsing with emotion. And coming off of the sword in waves was an otherworldly *heat.* The sword had always emitted a cool indifference. Now it was raging.

"Oh, God," Grace gasped. Her breathing sped up even more, and black began to edge in on her vision.

Something had angered this inanimate object. Fear, so familiar and yet, in this case, so different, choked Grace's throat. She had a gut feeling that in completing her job she betrayed a secret. The sword's secret.

Someone was coming. Coming for them. Coming for her.

She had one thought before losing consciousness: *What have I done?*

Chapter Two

Such rage.

It was one of the few emotions Jayden had felt in his entire existence, and it was burning him up from the inside out.

Scenery flashed by. Trees that were miles apart zoomed along in seconds. He had to get there. It was his own foolish fear—another unwelcome emotion—that allowed this to happen in the first place.

Between the two—rage and fear—he much preferred the rage. He had been around since the beginning of time, and never once abandoned his post. He had carried out his mission each time a human had dared defile the Trees, his sword making swift justice. And then, five humans had encroached on holy land. Jayden had sensed their looming connection to *her* and…run like a weak little human, the fear of encountering her much worse than anything Jayden could have imagined.

His failure filled his mouth like bitterest poison. Pure weakness. It was bad enough that his post was the laughing stock of heaven; Jayden was a warrior who never fought—it had been centuries since a human had stumbled upon the Garden. But, when given the chance to engage in battle, he actually *fled?* He would never forgive himself, but he *would* make it right. He would never hesitate to carry out his orders again.

When he had felt the immortal dying, Jayden bordered on hope. The thought that maybe he would not *have* to hunt them down—maybe they would kill themselves off as humans had been doing for millennia—had been drug-like in its euphoria. He could avoid her. Never even have to *see* her. It could be his salvation.

And then he had sensed the moment when the immortal healed. Because they used the fruit—again—to save him.

Jayden's roar of vengeance crashed out of his chest, startling wildlife and echoing off of mountains.

They had used the Trees again. Unforgivable. And he would make sure they knew it, just as soon as he could get his hands on his sword once more. The sword he had abandoned with his post to avoid his Temptation.

He reached the edge of land in Europe, and his wings automatically flared from his back, allowing him to take to the air as he hit what the humans had named the Atlantic Ocean.

They should already be dead. It was his job. They defiled the most holy gift to humanity, and they had to perish as recompense. The rightness of his mission bolstered his wings, and Jayden put on a new burst of speed, covering the expanse of the ocean in mere minutes.

By the time he reached the east coast of the United States, night had long ago fallen, and the sun was beginning to rise.

Good, he would be able to catch them when they were asleep. Vulnerable. His mission would be completed within minutes, and then he could reclaim the Trees they had uprooted from their rightful spot, return them to the Garden, and go about his sentry duty as God intended.

And if he came across his Temptation—Jayden nearly stumbled as his feet reclaimed the earth, his wings returning to their hidden spot in his back. No, he would not even allow himself to think of her. She was nothing. Nothing to him; nothing to the world. *Nothing.* He would carry out his mission and leave, whether he saw her or not.

He was getting closer. He could feel the sword speaking to him. That he actually left it behind in his haste to flee—Lord of the Most High. A soldier abandoning his weapon? Unheard of. At least amongst the *good* soldiers anyway. He crossed over the city of Washington, D.C., barely paying heed to the damage his burst of rage had laid out. He followed the sword's beckoning to an abandoned field and a conspicuous building that proclaimed loudly that it was a product of human government. This was the epicenter of his wrath, and it showed. The building was falling apart in the wake of what the humans would attribute to an earthquake. What had been a glass dome had exploded, allowing Jayden easy access. He quickly unfurled his wings and floated up and into the building.

He landed in a deathly quiet, wide-open room that held the Trees at its center. They grew from the dirt ground to fill the entire space. Their branches brushed against the outer walls; they sagged heavily with fruit.

They were beautiful.

Jayden realized with a start that, if he could miss anything, he would have missed these trees. They were the Most High's first gift to man; and the first gift that man had misused—just as they did with all of the Most High's gifts.

His eyes took in the damage to the room, and he barely stifled a wince as he saw fatalities on the floor. Fatalities that *his* anger caused. Reminders that he should be above emotion. He pushed the thought aside before it could manifest itself in more of the emotion that had visited Jayden twice already this day.

A wave of energy pulled his eyes from the trees. His sword was here. He could feel the sword responding to his arrival, waves of recognition rolling over him. He turned to his left, knowing that was where he would find it, and was pulled up short.

The sword was lying on a table, its red and black flames reflecting Jayden's wrath, but that was not what captured his attention.

Slumped on the ground below the table amid the sparkle of shattered glass was *her*. His Temptation.

Jayden hissed in a breath and took a stumbling step back, his eyes never straying from her form. She had a mass of curly red hair that was haphazardly piled on her head, writing utensils protruding here and there. She wore a pair of glasses with thick, black frames that hid most of her face, but Jayden could still see her lush eyelashes and pert, upturned nose. Her face was gently rounded. Feminine. His eyes zeroed in on her full, parted lips before sweeping the rest of her form. She was a curvy, soft woman. Her clothes, completely lacking a shape, did nothing to hide her sweet body from his observation. The humans today would immediately dismiss her as overweight or even plain, but to Jayden she was…*perfection*.

His Temptation.

Jayden groaned and took a stumbling step forward. She *would* be what he couldn't resist. That was the point. Since the Fall of Lucifer, every son of God knew that they would encounter a Temptation at some point in their immortal lives. Other than succumbing to Temptations, the only other way a son of God could Fall was partaking of the Tree of Eternal Life. And no angel would ever do that. Temptations were the heavenly realm's greatest threat. They could take several forms—Lucifer's had been power—but most often, a son of God faced his Temptation in a daughter of man. And she inevitably brought about his downfall. The daughters of man were forbidden. Every angel knew that. And yet—

Here was Jayden, standing over his lovely Temptation, aching with each breath to reach down and touch her.

He had severely underestimated the pull she would have on him. He had been right to flee when he felt her impending connection with the men who stumbled upon the Garden. He should have never come. Eventually, the Most High would have sent someone in his place to carry out his orders, but Jayden's pride—another emotion he should have denied himself—had driven him here.

She moaned and then turned over, her eyelashes fluttering.

Jayden watched in rapt horror as her eyes opened and gazed at him in unfocused confusion. They were gray. Stormy. Breathtaking. "*No*," he whispered fiercely as he felt something inside of him shift. He was doomed. He would *never* be able to leave her. He needed her so badly. Ached for her.

His arm stretched out from his side and toward her. He watched in disbelief as his fingers spread, yearning for the feel of her skin. Jayden never touched a human for any purpose other than death. What would it feel like to skim the pads of his fingertips down her cheek? He was suddenly breathless to know, an odd ache settling in the pit of his stomach. He bent toward her—

Those wide, unfocused gray eyes grew sharp in an instant. Confusion disappeared from their depths to be replaced with the terror Jayden had first been expecting. Seeing the terror in her eyes, however, devastated him on a scale he could not comprehend.

She gasped and lurched to a seated position, immediately scrambling back, not heeding the damage she was doing to her palms as they pounded through broken glass. Her back hit the desk, and she had nowhere else to go. She was taking her air in big, echoing gulps, and Jayden worried that she would lose consciousness again or harm herself further in her attempts to escape him.

"Calm, human," he commanded in a low voice made harsher than he intended by the thought of her leaving him.

"Go away," she ordered softly, yet fiercely.

Jayden frowned.

"Go away *now*!" Her voice was rising in panic. He could sense her heart rate speeding with fear. Her beautiful eyes were rolling around without finding purchase. Her shoulders slackened, her eyes grew dazed once more, and Jayden knew she was seconds from fainting.

He crouched down in front of her, reaching for her again to do—he knew not what. He only knew he felt this uncontrollable urge to calm her. To help her.

But at the sight of his hand reaching toward her, she whimpered and cowered even more. "No," she moaned. "Please…not…again." A small sob escaped her lips, and she clamped them shut, all color draining from her face.

Again? His Temptation made no sense.

"Grace?"

Jayden's hand had been stretching toward her, but at the sound of a man's voice behind him, his hand immediately reached over his Temptation's head and wrapped around the hilt of his sword. In less than a second, he whirled around, his back to his Temptation, sword at the ready, his body in a battle stance, coiled to attack. He would kill any threat to her.

Standing at the entrance to the room were two humans, a man and a woman. The man was very tall for a human. He had blond hair and light blue eyes that were focused on them with concern. At his side was a petite, dark-skinned woman with long black hair.

"Oh, thank God," he heard his Temptation whisper at the very moment he realized he was looking at two immortals, two defilers of the Trees. And then the fact that his Temptation's voice dripped with relief washed over him. She was *relieved* that these two abominations had come. Had stopped him from touching her.

A growl erupted from his chest, and he launched to a full upright position. He had orders to carry out. No humans were to touch the Tree of Eternal Life. These two had. It was his job to kill them and restore balance. He would finally fulfill his purpose. Finally fight.

He began to walk toward them slowly, sending out mental sensors toward the two defilers. He probed their minds easily. In an instant, he knew that the man had not partaken of the fruit willingly. Images of human testing and gut-wrenching sorrow flitted through Jayden's mind as his target's past became known to him. But the woman—Jayden's eyes landed on her, and he tilted his head to the side as he approached. *She* had willingly eaten the fruit. Had taken it with selfish motives—as part of a scheme of hers. Of the two of them, she was the more abhorrent.

She would die first.

The man must have seen some change in Jayden's eyes because he pushed the woman to her knees and stepped in front of her. Jayden didn't slow his approach. He reached them and with a swift palm to the chest, sent the man flying across the room. Jayden heard him hit the wall with a crack of bone and paid no further attention to him. It would take a few minutes for him to heal, giving Jayden more than enough time to dispatch the woman and make his way over to where the other defiler was.

The small, dark-skinned woman looked up at him, her eyes narrowing with a rage that matched Jayden's own. He was momentarily surprised—he expected fear—but lifted his sword all the same.

He heard a rush of fabric off to his left, but his sword was already moving.

"No!" his Temptation shouted as she stepped between his sword and the kneeling woman. "She's preg—"

It happened too quickly for Jayden to stop. He had been aiming low and for the crouched defiler's neck—a quick death, far more merciful than she deserved—but where her neck had been, his Temptation now was.

As his sword slid into her belly, her words cut off with a gurgle. Her eyes widened with disbelief and then narrowed as the pain of her wound hit her.

It was a mortal wound. Just as he had intended.

Jayden gaped as his Temptation tried to speak. A burble of blood ran over her bottom lip, and her legs failed her. The defiler behind her caught her as she sank to the ground.

"Grace!" The man he sent flying across the room now sprinted toward them. Jayden stumbled back as he watched them try to stem the flow of blood, his Temptation's life force spilling over their hands.

Fear. The emotion returned to him, and it was so severe it stole his breath. He felt a tremor begin in his legs and spread to his hands. He was *losing* her—just as he met her. He heard a moan of abject pain and realized it came from him. "No…"

The woman he intended to kill turned accusing eyes on him. "What the *fuck* are you?"

He did not answer. He only watched as the blood flow from the wound *he* had caused began to slow. His Temptation's eyes started to glaze.

"No!" he said again, scanning the room. His gaze landed on the Tree of Eternal Life. His wings sprang from his back, and he was flying toward it without another thought.

Chapter Three

It hurt. *God*, it hurt so bad.

And why were they pushing on it so hard? Touching her. Jericho and Dahlia's hands were weapons themselves, adding to her agony as they applied pressure to the gaping wound marring Grace's gut.

She tried to tell them to stop, was sure that she had, but she only tasted blood on her tongue.

That *thing*—the most beautiful, terrifying being she had ever seen—had…killed her. She was dying.

And maybe that was okay. She was so tired of being afraid. Of looking for someone to hurt her around every corner. She wasn't afraid right now, and it was the first time that'd happened in years. It almost made the pain worth it.

Almost.

Cold. Her teeth started to chatter. With a rush of relief she realized she could no longer feel their hands upon her. Her body was going blessedly numb.

But it was so cold.

Dahlia scooped her up into her arms and cradled her against her chest, rubbing her hands up and down Grace's arms. "Shh," she said. "It'll be over soon, Red. Shh…." Grace was still conscious enough to struggle, but when her efforts were unsuccessful, she realized her numb body did not react to Dahlia's touch as it always reacted to human contact. Without the ability to feel the pain of Dahlia's touch, Grace was shocked to discover that the other woman's embrace was…pleasant. It was the first time someone had put their arms around her in—she couldn't remember. A sudden, intense desire to live roared through her, and Grace tried to fight, to say something. But instead of a sound, her efforts brought another rush of blood.

The strength left her limbs, and she sagged into Dahlia's lap. Black began to edge in on her vision, so Grace closed her eyes to prevent watching it.

Dahlia tucked Grace's head into the curve of her neck and began to hum something soft and sweet. Grace smelled cinnamon. She relaxed. If she had to go—

As her senses dimmed, she heard a scuffle.

"Get *away* from her!" Jericho yelled. "Let her go in peace, for God's sake."

"She needs this," said a voice Grace had only heard twice but immediately recognized as *his*. "Now! *Right* now—"

A heavy silence met his insistence, and Grace wondered for a second if she had slipped away into death, but then she felt slices of renewed pain that must mean Dahlia was laying her down again.

The fear that had abandoned her for a few blessed moments rushed back in. What were they doing? She had no way of knowing.

"*Quickly*," she heard him say again, desperation dripping from his voice in a near moan.

Another rustle, and then the sweetest scent she'd ever encountered. A mix of peach and sun-warmed earth and sky. She tried to hum in approval, but cut off when she felt a curious sensation where the sword had sliced through her. It started off as a trickling tickle, but soon grew uncomfortably warm. It launched throughout her entire body, causing her back to bow.

She opened her mouth, and her scream rent the air. No flow of blood accompanied it this time, she realized dimly, as her limbs flinched and jerked on their own.

All pain disappeared and in its place was *ecstasy*. Pleasure like nothing she had ever felt warmed her to the tips of her fingers and toes. She moaned loudly as she turned to her side and curled in on herself. Her hands encountered the torn fabric of her blouse and jacket, but then felt smooth skin where moments ago had been carnage. The pleasure faded, and her fingers tentatively explored her abdomen.

The wound was…*gone*.

She opened her eyes to a world that was a blur. Colors blended with colors, shapes with shapes. Her fingers rose trembling to her eyes and bumped against her glasses. On instinct she whipped them away, and the world fell into immediate focus. She saw her surroundings with a clarity she had never known before; a clarity she instinctually knew was greater than human capability.

She was lying in a pool of her own blood, its vivid red color causing her to jerk upright. She looked around slowly. Jericho and Dahlia peered at her with cautious hope. "What—?" Grace's hoarse voice gave out.

A harsh noise behind her caught her attention. "You're alive," *he* said on an exhalation of breath.

She jerked around, her eyes finding him immediately.

He stood close—too close—and his eyes roved over her in a way that could only be described as proprietary. He was *gorgeous*. He had the beautiful dusky coloring of the exotic Middle East: mouthwatering dark skin, warm black hair that cascaded in waves around his shoulders. She craned her neck back to take in his stature. He was huge—tall and broad—but instead of being terrified, she reveled in his height and the wings that spread behind him and glimmered in the glow of the emergency lights. She sucked in a breath as she glanced over the wide expanse of his chest and down the flowing white robe that covered his body. Her gaze traveled back to his face and was snared by lush, full lashes framing light, honeyed-green eyes.

"Angel…" she heard herself mutter.

And then the world tilted violently as a soft, strong Voice whispered inside her mind: *He's yours. The One.*

• • •

Jayden felt the exact moment his Temptation connected with him for all eternity. It was a phenomenon he had only witnessed once, but one he immediately recognized in her wide, dazed eyes and parted lips. He was hers now. Her mate. He trembled. *At least that was what she would think,* he corrected himself.

Pure, unadulterated fear coursed through him for the third time in his life; however, this fear was much worse, much more intense than anything he had felt so far. If she paired with him, she would want him. Badly. He had only been in her presence for a handful of heartbeats, and already his self-control was severely tested. His was facing his Fall, and only one solution presented itself to him. Using the fear as fuel, he spun on his sandaled heel, and sprinted toward the door. He would leave. Simply leave her. Abandon his duty, *again.* But it was the only way he could save himself.

He heard the humans moving around behind him, shouting angry questions, but he paid them no heed. His only focus was on escape. He made it to the spot by the wall where he had first landed, and unfurled his wings with a violent *snap.* He crouched to take off, but couldn't move.

His brows drew together. He gathered his energy once again, crouched, and tried to launch himself from the floor, over the wall, and into the night.

Nothing.

It was as though he hit an imaginary wall.

With a roar, he spun around and pinned his Temptation with a glare. This was *her* fault. He needed to be away from her, and now that he had seen her, he could not leave her. He thought his brothers had been exaggerating when they warned him about the pull Temptations had on the sons of God. They undersold everything.

He growled low and bared his teeth before realizing he was behaving worse than an animal. The humans shrank back from him, their eyes wide. And that was the first time since giving her the fruit that he truly *looked* upon his Temptation.

He felt his mouth go slack; his breath left him in a rush. He stumbled toward her and then broke into a quick walk, never letting his eyes stray from their target.

The fruit had changed her. She was beautiful before, but now…. His mouth went dry, and that ache in his belly grew almost unbearable. Her features had realigned into perfect symmetry. Her body had gained strength right before his eyes. Though some of her weight had melted away, she was still lusciously curved, and Jayden was thankful for that. Those storm-cloud eyes swept over him from top to bottom and back to top, lingering over certain areas—he did not miss how she hungrily gazed at his chest—before settling on his eyes.

He was nearly bowled over by her emotions, not even needing to probe her mind. A wave of intense longing, so much more than lust, washed over him. But it only lasted two heartbeats before her revulsion followed on its heels. And it was her revulsion that caused him to remember himself.

Lord in Heaven, what had he just done? Given of the Trees to a *human*? The very thing he had been charged with correcting. And then, out of *fear*, he had tried to flee. Millennia of being the warrior who never fought, and he had run yet again when the chance presented itself.

He felt his lips curl into a snarl, his teeth gnash, but he stoutly resisted giving in to another emotion. He would not feel. Not anymore. Not again. He would not. He wanted to be angry with *her*, but he knew whose fault this was. He had felt her acceptance of death and rebelled against it with every fiber of his being.

His *Temptation*—she was aptly named.

He sneered at them all: his Temptation, huddled on the ground in a pool of her own blood; the woman defiler kneeling behind her; and the man, standing slowly and facing Jayden with a dangerous expression.

"You fucking bastard. You tried to kill my *wife*?" the man asked. The words began calmly enough, but escalated to a bellow. The wife in question stared at her mate with shock that betrayed how rare it was for the giant blond to use such language and such a tone.

"Yes," Jayden answered simply. Despite his attempt to ignore his Temptation, the scent of her blood was filling his nostrils and distracting him, reminding him of both his actions and how close he had come to losing her. "Get her out of those clothes. Cleaned up," he snapped at the blond's mate. He needed to think. Regroup. And he would not be able to do that with his Temptation covered in her own blood and crouched on the ground before him.

Pounding feet sounded behind him, and Jayden looked over his shoulder at the same moment everyone else focused on the door.

"Abilene's fine—" Another tall man—this one with dark hair and blue eyes—swung into the room and skidded to a halt as his eyes took in the scene they created. "What the hell? *Grace?*" He flew into a sprint, rushing past Jayden without another look and diving toward the two women huddled on the floor.

His Temptation threw herself back, away from the man's outstretched hands. Jayden frowned just as she opened her mouth: "Please, don't—"

"Do not touch her."

All four of their heads snapped around to stare at him, and Jayden realized *he* had said that. He snarled at them again, and his

Temptation shrank back. He fought against a wave of annoyance that her fear pinged against his mind.

He saw the new addition to their party take in Jayden's presence. The wings, the robe—it did not take a genius. He saw the man's blue eyes dip to the sword Jayden clutched in his right hand. "Okaaaay," he said slowly, coming to his feet with his hands spread wide. "I think I'd like to know what's going on here."

Jayden closed his eyes—something he never had to do to focus—as he reached toward the man's mind with his own, seeking his history: repeated torture, death, love, redemption. This defiler had experienced much. He had to die, but he was not a contender for the top of the list. That still went to the woman crouched behind his Temptation. Yet, his Temptation had said something as she stepped in front of Jayden's blade.

He forced himself to look into her eyes again, bracing for the hated emotions such an action would stir up. With gritted teeth, he asked, "Why?"

Her eyes widened at being addressed, but she did not need to ask for clarification. She knew exactly what Jayden was asking. Her chin shot up, and she pinned him with an imperious glare. "She's pregnant, you monster," she said, her gray eyes sharpening into daggers.

Jayden clenched his jaw. Nothing about that statement settled well with him. *Monster?* Did she really think of him as such? He shook his head, forcefully displacing such ridiculous thinking. It mattered not. But if the defiler was pregnant, Jayden had almost made a very serious error.

He closed his eyes again, focusing this time on the small woman who would be the first to die.

And there it was: a tiny, rapid heartbeat.

He had missed it. Heavenly Father, he had *missed* it.

He took a step back, turning from them slightly, his hand to his forehead rubbing the ache between his brows. The humans began to talk all at once, questions flying every direction.

"Silence," he ordered sharply, and was thankful when they immediately obeyed. He took a deep, calming breath and reevaluated the situation. An angel must always make sure to focus before allowing the Compulsion to set. Mistakes had been made in the past—angels who had gone rogue, believing themselves to be in the right. The Compulsion began when the angel finalized his plan, whether or not the angel's mission came down from the throne of the Most High. Thankfully, Jayden did not have to worry about that; he *knew* his mission came directly from the Most High. He only needed to make sure his plan would honor that being.

Inside this building were four—he corrected himself with an almost-wince—*five* immortals: the two men, and three women. His mind sifted hopefully through the information on the men. Both had been coerced into taking the fruit, but had eventually *willingly* signed over their compliance. They would be toward the top of the list. His mind also informed him that another of the immortals was pregnant. She lay in a different part of the facility nearing the end of her term. She had *not* willingly partaken of the fruit, but had had it forced upon her. She would be near the bottom. And then there was his Temptation.

The bottom, he immediately decided. *The very bottom of the list.* Agony clenched his gut as the full consequence of his actions hit home. He had single-handedly ensured that he would have to slay his own Temptation. Literally.

The sword in his hand flared momentarily as it echoed Jayden's dismay.

Free will was a gift the Most High only gave to the humans. Jayden *would* carry out his mission once it was decided. It was only a matter of time before the Compulsion took over.

He turned to the woman he deemed as the most vile. Yes, she was still at the top of the list, but the innocent she was growing inside of her put her firmly off limits. For now.

He narrowed his eyes. She had seven months remaining of a ten-month term. Would that be too long?

His eyes flicked over to his Temptation before he could stop them. Could he put the Compulsion off for seven months?

It was possible. He had already delayed deciding upon his mission for eight years. *But that had been when you knew they were seeking for a way to kill the defilers and daily putting it into practice.* Jayden grimaced. And those eight years had taxed him. He could no longer delay finalizing the plan that would trigger the Compulsion's count down. And once he did, the last eight years would weigh heavily. Seven additional months might be asking too much.

His mind sifted through the other three immortals on the planet—the ones everyone thought had never been created but had been disposed of when the two men before him had been turned by eating the fruit. He could go to their location. Kill them right now. It would buy him several precious months.

His mind immediately rejected it. No, those three men were as much to blame as the two before him, and therefore could not be slain any earlier. Besides, they were imprisoned. No immediate threat. The five before him were free. Roaming the earth. *Procreating.* Sanctioning more misuse of the Trees.

They were the greater threat.

His reasoning was done. His mission rolled out in his mind. Eight would die: the dark-skinned woman, the blond man, the blue-eyed man, the three imprisoned immortals over the sea, the other pregnant defiler—Jayden swallowed—and his Temptation.

He felt the certainty of it lock into place. His mission was set in stone. The clock began to count down. At some point—and Jayden didn't know when—it would become impossible to put off, and he would blindly go through the list, slaying them one by one. The only divergence would be if the first woman had not delivered yet. In that case, he would blindly move to the blond man and come back to the first woman when she had delivered.

He would blindly kill *her*. Jayden closed his eyes. Would spill her blood. Would watch the life drain from those beautiful gray eyes all over again.

So let it be done.

That was his duty, he reminded himself. He would *not* become like those of his brothers who Fell to their Temptations. Their love made them weak.

Love made them all weak.

He felt the blue-eyed man move and whipped around, his sword unfailingly finding the vulnerable point beneath the man's chin.

His mind told him the man's name was Eli, but Jayden quickly discarded the information. He did not want to know their names. He filtered through them one at a time, replacing their names with acceptable, distant modes of address: Eli became the "blue-eyed one"; Jericho, the "blond one"; Abilene, the "delicate one"; and Dahlia, the "mouthy one."

The blue-eyed one froze where he had been reaching for Jayden's sword.

"I would not advise that," Jayden said shortly, knowing it was only the man's position as third most viable threat that kept Jayden's sword from ending him now. He lowered the sword as the man stepped back, but the defiler's blue eyes flicked to a spot over Jayden's shoulder.

Jayden's muscles tensed just as the sound of gunfire lit the room. His left shoulder jerked forward, and Jayden stared down at a blooming spread of red right above his left pectoral. He felt no pain; he never did. But he *did* feel that calm adrenaline rush all warriors experienced in the heat of battle. The defilers before him huddled toward the floor, the blond one and blue-eyed one sheltering the women with their bodies in a move that Jayden would not have expected but could not help but approve.

Jayden turned to face the attack in a lazy spin. He could tell his utter lack of an emotional response made the attackers wary as he met their eyes. It was only a small group of men: three soldiers, covered in dust from the earthquake, each armed with a deadly automatic assault rifle.

Deadly to man, that is. And Jayden was not a man.

He lowered his chin and tightened the grip on his sword, and their gunfire stuttered to a stop. They had only hit him once, which meant they were not aiming to kill. He supposed he could return the favor.

He raised his left hand to chest height, stretched out before him. From the flat of his palm, he sent a blast of energy toward the three men. They fell back like trees in a storm, their weapons shooting from their hands and skittering across the floor as they fired ineffectually into the air. The blast robbed the three attackers of consciousness.

He turned back to the defilers just as nonchalantly as he had turned from them. All four gazed up at him with varying expressions of horror. He felt *her* eyes upon him, and avoided staring back at her, though he hungered to do so.

What was he going to do with these humans for seven months? He could not continue to let them wander free. For one thing, they were vile defilers. For another, letting them out of his sight would only trigger the Compulsion, and Jayden desperately wanted to delay that for as long as possible. He told himself it was for thousands of reasons, none of which involved a reticence to kill his Temptation.

He frowned. He had no place to store five humans for seven months. Cherubim did not own compounds. But he *was* currently standing in the midst of a compound in disarray—

He flicked the sword to the left, toward the area of the facility where he knew the delicate one lay in bed. "Move now or die now," Jayden said simply and in a level voice. "The choice is yours."

When they all blinked up at him wordlessly, Jayden reached forward and grabbed the blond one by the collar of his shirt and jerked him to his feet. "Die now, it is," Jayden said, pressing the blade of his sword to the man's throat and fighting a sick feeling climbing his throat as he prayed he could stop with just this one. The blade shimmered in the glow of the lights.

"No!" the mouthy one yelled, shooting to her feet and dragging his Temptation to hers as well. "We'll move. We'll move!" She was screaming the words at him in near hysteria, and Jayden barely refrained from shaking his head.

Weak.

"That's right," the blue-eyed one said, his hands spread out wide in a placating manner. "We're moving right now."

Jayden shrugged as he willed his heart to slow and released the blond one. "Now or later," he said with forced calm. "The outcome will be the same." He flicked his sword toward the exit one more time, and this time, all four humans made their way to the door with urgency.

They entered the wing where the other defiler was located, and shocked mortals stopped in their path as they stepped around rubble and stared at the picture they made. Without having to receive any more direction, the defilers made their way to the delicate one's room and filed in without a word. Jayden stood in front of the door, barring their exit, and turned to face the mortals lurking in the hall. "Get out," he said softly. The majority of them needed no convincing; their already frazzled nerves from the earthquake had them running toward the exit. But one or two remained in the hallway, gawking at the blood-soaked angel. Jayden reached out and snatched the one closest to him, tossing him toward the exit, and the rest took the hint, sprinting away as quickly as their inferior bodies could carry them.

When Jayden saw no more mortals, he tilted his head to the side and sent telepathic feelers out to the remaining rooms in the wing. Satisfied that no one else remained in this part of the building, he sent another blast of energy toward the entrance to the wing. The earth rumbled, and giant pieces of the already weakened ceiling began to crack and fall to the ground. In seconds, the wing was closed off from the world, a mountain of debris sealing them in.

He turned around to find all five defilers glaring at him.

He met every glare. "You five are my prisoners from now until the moment you die."

He created this problem. He would contain it until the end. He could easily defend this fortress of a facility from outside interference.

"Your *prisoners?*" the blond one asked.

"Like hell!"

They erupted into a cacophony of mindless arguments that Jayden paid no heed to while the delicate one asked what was going on in a small, scared voice from her bed.

Jayden saw nothing but his Temptation. Something in her expression both beguiled and worried him. She seemed to be focused on a burden all her own, one that had nothing to do with being trapped in a building with four humans and an angel. Jayden watched as she opened her mouth and spoke softly to the room at large.

"Excuse me," she whispered.

The others did not hear her. They were too busy arguing with each other and yelling at him.

"*Excuse me!*" she shouted.

The four stopped mid-word and turned to face her.

Her hand trembled as it shoved her unruly red hair from her eyes, and her thoughts were embroiled with the words she had received from the Most High right after turning immortal. Her gray eyes flicked Jayden's direction for a moment, as though she already suspected what the answer would be, before asking, "What does *The One* mean?"

Their mouths all dropped open. As a unit, their heads all swiveled in Jayden's direction.

The mouthy one was the first to react. "Oh, *shit*."

Chapter Four

Grace's world narrowed down to her worst nightmare. Grace stared at Dahlia and Abilene with a hand over her mouth. "Please tell me you're kidding," she begged through her fingers.

She was sitting next to Dahlia at Abilene's bedside. They were locked in, the door the most secure modern technology could provide. They all knew it provided no protection whatsoever.

As soon as the words *The One* left her mouth, things had changed. Her simple question garnered an immediate and intense result. Eli had turned on the angel, shouting, "What did you do to her?" Jericho had placed a hand on his friend's shoulder in a vain attempt to calm him, and Dahlia had ordered, "Men, out!" so fiercely that even the angel had not hesitated to obey. And then had come the earth-shattering news. Dahlia explained *everything*. Words Grace never wanted to hear spoken aloud—orgasm, touch, excruciating pain—peppered every sentence. When Grace had looked upon the angel after the fruit turned her, she had Impulse-paired with him. They were now mates, and as Dahlia continued to describe everything that would entail, Grace nearly suffocated from panic. She found herself near hyperventilation toward the end when she was told she was going to have to *touch herself*, to bring herself to orgasm, to avoid what Dahlia and Abilene both called "a pain worse than death."

They spoke this so easily, as though it weren't completely shattering. Sure, bring herself to orgasm. Avoid pain. They didn't realize that sex and pain were inextricably twined in Grace's mind. She hadn't touched herself since *it* happened. Years without a single orgasm. And that was just the way she liked it. "Impulse-paired?" Grace repeated in a dead voice to the two women who were so happy in love it was obnoxious. "Like you two did with Eli and Jericho?" Their happiness could never be hers, and they couldn't seem to recognize that.

Dahlia exchanged a glance with Abilene while the baby's heartbeat echoed steadily from the many monitors in the room. "Well," Dahlia said, "I wouldn't say *exactly* like we did. We weren't held prisoner by a crazy man with a vendetta."

Abilene smiled weakly and shifted with a wince, her hand smoothing over her protruding belly. "Speak for yourself."

"Huh," Dahlia said, squinting her eyes. "I guess that's right. Come to think of it, Jericho kinda held me prisoner, too." She looked at Grace again. "Forget what I said. This is totally normal."

Grace launched herself from her seat. "*Normal?* I've Impulse-paired with a psycho," she ticked off the items on her fingers as she glared at the women, "I'm going to have to *touch* myself, and what's more horrifying, everyone knows it. Or, I let *the psycho* touch me." She didn't stop the shudder of revulsion. That last item was definitely not an option. "Oh, yeah. And we're being held prisoner by that same psycho until 'the moment we die,'" she dropped the tally to make air quotes with her fingers, "which is God knows how long—"

"Oh my God," Abilene interrupted, trying to sit up straighter. "I'm going to give birth in captivity, aren't I?" The heart rate monitor's beeping increased in pace.

Dahlia rolled her eyes. "Way to go, Red." Dahlia reached for Abilene's hand and gave it a squeeze. "Relax, Abi. None of us knows how long the angel plans on keeping us."

"What am I going to do? I'm the only doctor. I can't deliver my own baby!" The heart rate didn't slow.

Some of Grace's rage abated, and her energy whooshed out of her like wind leaving sails. "I'm sorry—" Grace began.

Dahlia cut her off. "You don't get to talk for a second." She turned back to Abilene, her other hand moving to cover hers where it clenched on her belly. "Relax, Abi. Shhh…Going into labor now is not the best idea, okay?"

Abilene focused on Dahlia's face, and the words seemed to penetrate because she nodded, closed her eyes, and focused on breathing deeply.

The beeps slowed, and Dahlia and Grace breathed a simultaneous sigh of relief. Grace opened her mouth to speak, but Dahlia shook her head. "If the time comes, you'll tell me what to do, and I'll do it. Okay? Everything will be fine." Her slim, brown fingers moved to Abilene's hair, and she ran them through the blond ringlets over and over again and Abilene's breathing relaxed.

The poor woman, a full two weeks past due, was always exhausted. It wasn't long before she fell into deep slumber.

Grace took her seat by Dahlia again as the woman leaned back and let out a breath. "I really am sorry," Grace felt the need to say again.

Dahlia turned to her. "For what? This isn't your fault."

Wish I could agree. Everything about this felt like her fault. Something told her that their captor was far too interested in Grace for their imprisonment to be an accident.

"Now," Dahlia said, drawing Grace from her thoughts. "If I could get close enough to touch him, I could use the Knowledge. Find out if his intent is evil."

Raw jealousy flashed red behind Grace's eyes, and she made a noise that sounded feral. "You will not touch him," Grace growled.

Grace clapped a hand over her mouth with a gasp.

Dahlia raised an eyebrow, her fingers in Abilene's hair pausing for a moment. "Okay, see, *this* is what we were talking about, Red." Her brown eyes sharpened. "It's only going to get worse. You need to take care of things. The sooner the—"

"I can't do that," Grace said desperately, cutting Dahlia off mid-sentence.

Dahlia chuckled. "Relax. You might like it."

Grace made a gagging noise, and Dahlia's smile widened. "Or, hey, give the angel some payback for being an utter ass. Make *him* do it. One angel sex slave coming up," she said on a chuckle.

Dahlia's eyes immediately widened at whatever expression she saw on Grace's face. "Okay, bad joke," she said quickly, reaching for Grace with one hand.

Grace flinched away, nearly falling from her chair. She used the momentum to roll to her feet, something she never would have accomplished before, and launched herself into a pacing tirade at the foot of Abilene's bed. "Oh, God, oh, God, oh, God."

And then, Grace caught sight of her reflection in the glass of the door. She stopped dead in her tracks. "Oh, God," she said again, this time a whisper. Her fingers moved to the glass and traced her image. *I'm…pretty.* The thought had a curious effect: half elation, half dread. On the one hand, she had never been pretty before. Had never been noticed as such by the opposite sex. Never admired. On the other hand, she had never been pretty before. Had never, since that one time, been the kind of woman a man forced. No man had wanted to touch her. She'd made sure of it, enhancing her natural ugliness with a cultivated one.

The dread won. "This isn't happening," Grace shrieked, her voice rising. "God, I can't be *pretty!*" Her hands fell to her belly, which was notably smaller. Hysteria took over. "It's gone." Her breathing dissolved into hyperventilation. "My weight," she moaned.

"Hey, whoa," Dahlia said, rising to her feet and standing between Grace and the door's reflection. "Grace, what's happened to you?" Dahlia reached toward her.

Grace flinched away from Dahlia's hand, and worried her bottom lip at the flare of concern in Dahlia's warm eyes. *Should I tell her?* The desire to do so was completely foreign. She hadn't told anyone since the police report and unsuccessful trial, but it was suddenly ready to burst out of her. This was her worst nightmare. She was faced with touching herself, or even having someone else touch her. She needed help. "Dahlia," she began hesitantly, "I was—"

The door smashed open. Abilene started in the bed, and Dahlia was a blur as she spun around.

The angel stood in the doorway, menace radiating off of him in waves. His honey-green eyes pinned her with a stare that was completely indefinable, and Grace shrunk back, worried that he'd somehow overheard and guessed what she'd been about to say.

His wings weren't visible anymore, but his shoulders took up the entire door space. His robe shimmered in the low lighting. His hair flowed over his shoulders in waves.

Her betraying body lurched as feelings she'd never felt swarmed over her, the predominant one *lust*.

And then his eyes softened. He swept her body with a hungry look.

Boots sounded in the hallway, breaking the spell. Jericho and Eli elbowed past the angel, pinning him with reproachful stares. The angel tilted his head to the side as he stared right back at them. Then he suddenly spun around and stalked off leaving them all with baffled expressions on their faces.

Grace's confusion at the angel's sudden departure was overwhelmed by the flare of need he had ignited with that hungry look. She closed her eyes and wound her arms around her stomach. As she tried to hold herself together, she couldn't help but wish she'd died.

• • •

They were as easy to read as young children after forbidden sweets. Jayden shook his head, disappointed in the lack of challenge the defilers presented.

He wanted to hear whatever it was that his Temptation had been about to tell the mouthy one, but the men storming in with loud thoughts of escape forced Jayden to step outside and prepare for their plan.

Jayden reached the cave-in in seconds. He took up residence in the corner between wall and rubble, and slowly unfurled his wings—a move as close to a lazy stretch Jayden would ever get. He encircled himself with the iridescent feathers, immediately rendering himself invisible to the human eye.

He leaned back and crossed his arms over his chest and his legs at the ankle. Now, it was a waiting game. If their thoughts had been any indication, the men would not be able to wait long before acting on their idea.

A handful of moments later, the door to the delicate one's room swung inward without a sound.

Jayden never smiled, but nevertheless, he found it difficult to tamp down a surge of amusement. In the years that had passed since Jayden's last unfortunate—for the human anyway—encounter with man, Jayden had forgotten that they were a constant source of lowbrow entertainment, not too different from watching baby animals blunder around.

The blond one stuck his head out into the hallway and looked right and left. He made a gesture as he moved to stand beside the door. The blue-eyed one sprinted out the door and toward Jayden and the cave-in.

"Where is he?" the blue-eyed one hissed, reaching for a rock and silently setting it aside.

Jayden parted his wings and cleared his throat. Both men froze. "I believe I can answer that," Jayden said softly.

"Oh, hell," the blond one muttered from his post.

The blue-eyed one turned his head slowly until he met Jayden's gaze.

"I do not think I need to tell you that I could easily squelch this misbegotten escape attempt."

The blue-eyed one shook his head.

"Good. Now, return to your women and inform them of your failure."

Raw anger flared quickly in those blue eyes, and his thoughts screamed rebellion, but the man stared at Jayden without an audible word.

On the other side of the rubble, Jayden heard the whispers of many men. His temper frayed to the breaking point. A rescue attempt from both sides? These humans did not know what they played with.

The Compulsion throbbing within his skull, Jayden jerked forward and snatched the blue-eyed one to him with a hand around the throat.

"Hey, hey—" the blond one said in a voice half urgent, half soothing. With palms out, he took several steps toward where Jayden now squeezed the other human's neck.

"Stay where you are," Jayden barked as he struggled to get the Compulsion back under control. If those men on the outside burst through, that would be it. Jayden would lose himself and regain awareness amid horrible carnage. No one was safe.

A vein began to throb in the blue-eyed one's forehead, and still the man glared at Jayden with all the defiance he possessed. Against his will, Jayden felt a flare of respect stab through him.

He loosened his fingers slightly. The blue-eyed one sucked in a ragged breath.

Jayden would never be able to keep them here without them trying to escape. Without someone trying to rescue them. Unless—

Jayden abruptly dropped his hand. As the blue-eyed one folded over to clutch his knees and gasp, Jayden turned to the blond one. "How did the men on the other side know to meet you at the cave-in?"

The man's wary eyes hardened, and his chin kicked up a notch.

With a sigh, Jayden marched forward, intent on prying the information from him bodily before realizing from the man's thoughts that he would not cave to physical intimidation. Jayden turned once more toward the blue-eyed one and reached for him again—

"Okay, okay!" the blond one shouted.

Jayden let his arm fall to his side and faced the blond one once more with a raised eyebrow.

"We've been in contact through cell phone."

Ah, yes. The humans were never far from their gadgets. Jayden stalked closer to the blond man whose Adams apple bobbed, though he did not step back.

"Listen to me now," Jayden said in a low voice once they were toe-to-toe, "and know that I do not lie. No human, not even a strong one, stands a chance against me. If there is a rescue attempt—from *either* side—again, you are all dead. You *and* the innocents who would attempt to aid you."

No reaction from either man.

"Your women as well." Jayden looked directly into the blond one's eyes, the truth and horror of his statement as apparent as Jayden could make it. "You will set me off, and not even I will be able to stop myself."

Now the blond one reacted. "Don't you lay a hand on—"

Jayden cut him off with a raised palm. "Call them and tell them it is unsafe to attempt rescue."

Still the blond one hesitated.

"Do it," the blue-eyed one rasped from over Jayden's shoulder. The man's thoughts of his mate and unborn child mixed with panic and poured directly into Jayden's mind. Whatever the human heard in Jayden's voice, it was enough to convince him Jayden was as out of control as he probably was.

With fumbling fingers, the blond one pulled a slim phone from his pocket and made the call.

Jayden stretched forward his palm. "Give it to me."

As soon as the cool metal hit Jayden's skin, he crushed the phone within his fist. "That was the first wise thing you have done today. Return to your women. Enjoy the time you have left."

The door to the delicate one's room clicked shut behind the men, and Jayden had no problem overhearing what was said and thought within.

"—completely deranged—"

"Can turn invisible—"

That particular divulgence drew a unique blend of wistful and envious thoughts from his Temptation. *All* of them felt their situation was hopeless, even if they refrained from saying so out loud.

A few minutes later, they all dejectedly decided to call it a night. As the door opened once more, Jayden surrounded himself with his wings, so he could watch the defilers in stealth. The blond one and the mouthy one took an examining room a few doors further down without once looking in the spot they both knew Jayden was hidden.

His Temptation, however, stopped mid-stride and turned to look directly at Jayden. Her stare was so penetrating that Jayden's feathers ruffled as he strove to make sure he was fully covered.

She sighed from deep within her gut, and her thoughts hit Jayden full in the face: *Lucky angel.*

Without another thought, she continued to walk down the hall and into a room several away from everyone else.

She so desperately wanted to be invisible. For no one to see her. *Why?*

The Compulsion jerked within him. As though he felt a chill, Jayden tightened his wings around his body. But the movement was not enough to stop an errant, completely inappropriate thought: He would shield her from all other eyes forever, if only he could.

Chapter Five

The past twelve hours had not changed much, except for the humans' strategy. Jayden leaned against the wall outside the delicate one's medical room and listened unashamedly as they all talked in hushed tones within. Now, rather than escape, it sounded as though their plan were to "win him over."

Jayden scoffed. Terrible plan.

They began urging his Temptation to play off of their connection.

Jayden frowned. Maybe they were smarter than he thought. And Jayden obviously revealed more weakness where his Temptation was concerned than was acceptable.

No, Jayden shook his head. He had no weakness where his Temptation was concerned. He was resolute.

It did not matter anyway. His Temptation refused so violently, Jayden did not have to use any stealth to overhear.

Jayden sighed as he realized he automatically tensed at her refusal. It would only *help* matters if she vowed to stay away from him.

Then—through the walls, over their arguing—Jayden heard his Temptation's stomach growl.

He did not realize he moved until his hand slapped the cool metal door. He pushed it open, and it bounced off of the wall.

They all froze like naughty children, their eyes blinking at him widely.

"You need sustenance."

He was speaking only to his Temptation, but the mouthy one stepped forward. "Yes," she said in a light, lilting voice that differed greatly from the one she had used thus far. "That's a great idea. There are some MREs in the emergency supply closet. I could go get them."

Winning him over seemed to be in full effect. He realized that he had *again* shown concern for his Temptation and forced his face into a mask of indifference, with only a slight grimace. "It matters not to me." Jayden shrugged. "You will all die soon anyway. But suit yourself."

The mouthy one clicked her tongue and threw one hand up in the air as the other landed on her cocked hip. "Does he have to keep saying that?" She asked, turning to her mate. "I can't be nice to him if he says shit like that."

"Okay, okay," the blond one said stepping forward and ushering his mate out into the hall as quickly as possible. Probably afraid Jayden would kill her on the spot. He was tempted. "We'll be right back," he threw over his shoulder. Jayden heard them argue as they made their way down the hall.

The delicate one tried to give Jayden a dim smile from her bed, but he barely saw it. This was the first moment since her longing stare yesterday that Jayden had seen his Temptation. And right now his eyes were riveted.

When she noticed him looking at her, her gray eyes quickly darted away from a glazed focus on his wings. Her hair was more a tempest than it had been yesterday. Her clothes, still sliced and bloody from his sword, were even more rumpled today. She had discarded the jacket of her oversized business suit, and Jayden's eyes were caught by the flashes of smooth skin revealed by the barely-together garment. Her stomach was beautiful. Perfect. His hands itched to touch it, to slide across what was probably the softest thing he would ever touch.

She fidgeted under Jayden's stare. "Sh-she didn't mean it," she said softly.

It took a moment for Jayden to remember the mouthy one's casual insult. He could not focus on anything but his Temptation's body. "Yes she did," he replied automatically. Before his eyes, her nipples hardened, pressing into two distinct, perfect peaks. Jayden's mouth watered. His belly ached, much worse than it had yesterday. He placed an open palm over his lower abdomen and rubbed absently.

She crossed her arms over her middle and chest, breaking the spell. Jayden raised his eyes to her face and froze at the pure, unadulterated terror in their stormy depths.

Jayden sucked in a breath. He petrified her. He closed his eyes and focused. *No, not just me.* What she felt for him scared her, too.

She *wanted* him.

Everything she had just been thinking washed over him. He saw himself through her eyes. Saw as lust and awe flashed across his face while he watched her breasts harden. Felt her breathless longing.

He opened his eyes in shock, barely suppressing a groan at the depth of her desire. But then he focused on her eyes again. None of those emotions were there now. Only the terror. It poured off of her in waves.

Oh, she had wanted him for a moment, but that moment was long gone. Her fear was so stark he could nearly taste it. He found himself wishing to reassure her, tell her he would not hurt her.

But it would be a lie. And the cherubim could never lie.

The blond one and the mouthy one reentered the room, piles of MREs in their arms. They skidded to a stop and, as one, looked back and forth between Jayden and his Temptation. Without a word, the mouthy one moved to stand before Grace, her brows crashed down over her eyes.

Jayden blinked. He realized every muscle in his body was taut with tension. He had taken several steps toward his Temptation while his thoughts had been occupied, and his hands were fisted at his sides.

He forced himself to relax, once more making his face a blank mask. "She needs clothes," he ordered empirically. "I already told you so once. Get her some immediately. I do not want to see that," he gestured toward the general area of her exposed skin, "anymore."

Oddly enough, his words caused his Temptation's face to fall. A corresponding ache sharply flicked through his chest. Before he could make a greater fool of himself, he turned on one sandaled heel and left the room. As soon as he was out of sight, he fell against the wall in the sterile hallway, his breath leaving him in a whoosh.

Inside the room, the blond one asked, "What the hell was that?"

The blue-eyed one gave a vivid—and accurate—recounting of Jayden's reaction to his Temptation, making sure to leave nothing out. Jayden had completely forgotten the presence of the other two in the face of his Temptation's charms. He brought his hand to his forehead to smooth the tension there. His hand was shaking.

The Compulsion stretched within him like a predator preparing to strike. Jayden gritted his teeth and forced it back down. *Lord of the Most High, this cannot be over quickly enough.*

•••

"Grace."

I do not want to see that anymore.

Grace couldn't breathe, her chest hurt so badly. *I do not want to see that—*

"Grace."

She knew they were calling her, trying to talk to her. She couldn't make her mind track. Her eyes were stinging. That meant tears. And Grace knew if she started, she wouldn't be able to stop.

I do not want to see that. Grace rubbed her stomach through the gash in her shirt, trying to gauge just how horrifying her fat stomach actually was to look upon. It must be just as bad as it always had been, even though the fruit had caused her to drop so much weight. Weight she needed to hide behind; weight she loathed.

"*Grace!*"

Grace jumped, and the momentum caused one of the tears she'd been fighting to tip over the edge of her lower lid and trail down her cheek. Grace squeezed her eyes shut and held her breath, certain every second would be the last she maintained control.

You are beautiful, the Voice whispered to her mind.

Grace's eyes popped open. The Voice had been speaking to her constantly since the moment she found out that the angel was capable of invisibility. It whispered…*encouragements* to her. It was just unsettling enough to pull Grace from this latest dark reverie.

Her eyes focused to find all four of her fellow prisoners staring at her with varying expressions of concern and wariness. She focused on Dahlia, who was closest and had her mouth opened, as though she were going to say Grace's name again.

Grace took a shuddering breath. "What?"

Dahlia snapped her mouth shut. Apparently, now that she had Grace's attention, she didn't know what to do with it. After several seconds, "Are you okay?"

Grace breathed a disbelieving laugh.

The corner of Dahlia's mouth turned up fractionally. "Let's get you some clothes, okay?" she asked softly.

Grace let her eyes fall shut as she fought to keep from remembering just how disgusted the angel had sounded as he looked upon her exposed skin.

Grace, no, the Voice whispered. *You misinterpret—*

Grace's gasp interrupted the Voice. She snapped open her eyes. She *misinterpreted?* That was not something Grace did. *Ever.* She embraced the anger that overshadowed the shame. The Voice had to stop. It was creepy and weird, and she couldn't take any more changes right now.

She turned to Dahlia once more. "This Voice thing...."

Dahlia's eyes widened. "It's speaking to you?"

Grace nodded. It was all she was capable of as she tried to find a diplomatic way of asking how to make it go the hell away.

"Isn't it great?" Jericho asked, drawing Grace's eyes to him.

Grace felt one eyebrow rise and her lips pinch, but Abilene and Eli were too busy adding their like-minded comments for anyone to notice.

Dahlia, however, snorted, and all eyes turned to her. Grace felt a flare of comfort that was quickly squelched by the woman's next words: "Actually, it *is* pretty cool."

Et tu, Dahlia? Grace scowled. "What is it supposed to be, *God*?" Okay, even Grace recognized how bitchy that sounded. Proverbial crickets sounded in the aftermath, as everyone looked at her with mouths open.

Eli spoke first in calm, measured words. "Is that a problem?"

Grace swallowed hard, but refused to back down. "Come on. I'm an intellectual."

Now Eli was angry. "Whereas I'm dumber than dirt, so I'm *allowed* to think it's God?"

Abilene spoke up from the bed. "Okay, okay, corners, people." Her eyes held understanding as she looked at Grace. "Why does it matter if it's God, Grace?" she asked softly.

Grace felt her brow crinkle even further. "Oh, seriously, I can't be the only person in this room who's thinking it."

"Thinking what?" Jericho bit out in a low voice.

Grace sighed. Great. She'd pissed him off, too. "That if it's God—and it seems to *like* us—then why is there an *angel* here set on killing us?"

More crickets.

"Huh," said Dahlia. "How 'bout that?"

Eli clenched his fist. "That is—a really good question."

"Are we sure he's an angel?" Jericho asked.

"He's too much of a self-righteous asshole to be anything else," Dahlia muttered.

Grace sidled closer to Abilene's bedside as the other three continued to mull over this newest question.

"Don't worry," Abilene whispered. "It takes some getting used to, but soon you'll love it."

They were back to talking about the Voice. "Does it ever go away?" Grace couldn't keep herself from asking.

Abilene shook her head at the same time the Voice whispered, *I am always here.*

Grace had the feeling she was meant to be comforted by that. Instead, every muscle tensed. One of the few comforts Grace had was her solitude. Was even that to be taken from her?

I do not take, only give.

"Yeah, right."

Abilene smiled, and Grace realized she'd spoken out loud.

"Crap," Grace said.

Abilene giggled. "Don't worry. We all do that sometimes."

"—'bout to die of boredom."

Grace and Abilene turned toward the other three.

"We could clean up the wing from the earthquake," Jericho offered. "It would keep our hands busy at least. You know, with something other than throttling the angel."

Grace leapt at the opportunity. "I'll help." Anything to keep her distracted.

When Grace tried to follow them out into the hallway, Dahlia stopped her. "Let's get you some clothes first, all right?"

The words were said kindly, but that didn't keep Grace from flinching. *I do not want to see that anymore.*

"Oh, Grace, I didn't mean—" Dahlia reached out to touch her. Grace sidestepped, and Dahlia's hand hovered in the air.

"Right." Grace didn't even recognize her own voice. "Clothes. Of course."

Chapter Six

Grace lay in bed the next morning and stared at the drop-tile ceiling. She was in the room at the end of the medical wing, away from all of the others. There were a good three rooms between her and her nearest co-prisoners, Jericho and Dahlia.

She didn't think standing in a corner and hugging herself while wishing to be invisible would make this go away. Last night, after cleaning the wing, they sat through a tense communal dinner of liquid spaghetti and meatballs. And, though a nine-and-a-half month pregnant woman lay, literally, in their midst, they had all eyed *Grace* like she was a ticking time bomb.

For someone who was used to disappearing into the walls, it was very disheartening.

But not quite as disheartening as the brief flares of discomfort along her nerve endings that had sent her to bed at eight o'clock. No, *those* had been absolutely terrifying. As terrifying as Abilene's response to Grace's whispered question, "How bad will it get if I don't…"

Bad. Very *bad.*

Grace had the covers tucked up to her chin. Underneath the sheet, she wore only a baggy scrubs top, which hit her mid-thigh when she was standing, and a pair of no-nonsense panties. She turned her head and stared longingly at the one-size-too-big scrub bottoms meticulously folded over a chair. With every fiber of her being, she longed to put them on. To cover her new body—she estimated she was now a size 16—with frumpery and go on with her day as though nothing had happened.

But something *had* happened. Grace idly scratched her neck at a brief flare of hot, itching pain. It was worse today. The flares were closer together—already, since waking, Grace had experienced several of them. They showed up at random spots on her body. And always, accompanying the physical discomfort, her brain flashed images of the angel behind her eyes. His flowing, vibrant brown hair. The skin so warm and sweet in color she wondered if it tasted of raw sugar. Those eyes a color she'd never seen: honey-drenched moss. His height. His broad shoulders. The powerful body his robe did nothing to hide. His chest.

Her lips opened as her new, improved memory provided a perfect sensory recollection of his massive, beautiful chest. Flat planes of muscle that spread forever. Muscle she could sink her fingers into. Rest her cheek against. Nuzzle.

She squeezed her eyes shut and slapped a hand to her forehead. "Ugh, no!" she scolded herself. She held her breath until the unwelcome image began to have black dots pierce it. With a whoosh of air, she threw herself onto her side. She did *not* want to think of that *creature* as a sexual object. She hadn't thought of a man in that way since she was seventeen—too young, naïve, uneducated, and hormonal to know better.

Bad. Very *bad.*

For perhaps the millionth time since last night, Abilene's grave warning flitted through her head.

Grace heaved a sigh, and with her eyes squinched shut as tightly as possible, she put her right hand beneath the sheets. She began to trail it down her body slowly, giving her mind—already at the verge of panic—time to accept the inevitable: they were going to have to do this. Her fingertips passed through the valley between her breasts. Grace's skin began to crawl. They reached her soft, rounded belly. A fine tremor settled into Grace's arms. They reached the elastic band of her panties.

Grace's mind bailed ship.

"Seth, this isn't funny," she said, clutching her hands to her breasts and eyeing her boyfriend's best friend, Joe, where he stood silhouetted in the doorway. Whatever was going on, his addition to the private moment between Grace and her boyfriend was unwelcome.

Grace couldn't see his eyes in the darkness of the room, but she imagined they were glowering as Joe's dark form observed her where she lay half-naked on Seth's bed. "Wow, you got this far," he said to Seth with a sneer. "You sure you need my help for the rest?"

From where he sat beside her on the bed, Seth laughed the same vibrant laugh that had first gotten Grace to notice him. "Man, this is as far as she ever goes." Seth gestured Joe into the room. "Let's do this. I'm so ready for it to be over."

Grace tried to snatch the sheet over her body, but Seth was sitting on it, and he didn't budge. Dread was slowly fermenting in her stomach. "Um, I should go," she offered timidly. Both men turned to her like hawks spotting prey. "My roommate is expecting me."

They laughed, and then Joe entered the room, closed the door behind him, and clicked the lock into place. The snick of the gears shot through the last of Grace's hesitation and hopeful doubt. She jumped up from the bed where she and Seth had been kissing and touching only moments before, and snatched her shirt from the floor, making a beeline for the door.

Joe easily snatched her against his chest as she tried to push past him in the small dorm room and flung her back to the bed.

That was the moment when Grace fully realized that they were going to rape her. Her vision wavered, and she turned her eyes upon Seth as he stood from the bed and began to undo his jeans. "Why would you—" she swallowed down a panicked sob. "Seth…I love you. Don't do this."

Joe let out an abrupt bark of laughter. "Oh my God!" He clapped Seth on the back. "You're good, man, you're good. You got her to love you? That wasn't part of the deal. Shit, not even I'm that cruel."

Grace scrambled back on the bed and hit the wall with a thud.

"Shut the fuck up, man, and just grab her arms. Let's get it done." He made a noise of disgust. "Look at her. She's such a fat cow." He glanced down and Grace's eyes automatically followed, landing on his flaccid penis. She turned her face into the wall with a gasp. "How am I even going to get it up?" Seth asked.

Grace moaned, wondering why, with what was about to happen, his words were what were hurting her most. Like a child, she covered her head with her arms. Light shattered her attempt at hiding as her arms were jerked over her head. Joe held her down and said, "You'll figure something out, man. Picture someone else."

Seth laughed. "I always do with this one." Then he flopped himself down on top of her.

His hot breath fanned her face with the stench of cheap beer. Joe's excited breathing echoed behind her head; his fingers dug into her skin with unforgiving force. Grace turned her face into her shoulder as tears pooled in her ears, trying to ignore the fact that her pants were being yanked down her legs.

Seth shoved her legs apart with his knees. Horrid, gut-wrenching terror speared her at the foreign feeling of an erection pressing against her naked flesh.

"You're nothing," Seth whispered to her. "Nothing but a stupid bet."

He drove into her body, and after the first searing sting, the only thing she felt was the shattering pain of his hands on her body.

With a cry that neared a scream, Grace wrenched her hand out of her panties. She rolled violently to the side, finding air and then the unforgiving floor, pain shooting up through her knees and hands as she hit concrete.

For several heart-wrenching seconds, Grace thought she had lost all of the control she'd gained over the last thirteen years. The entire rigor she'd put her mind through. All of the knowledge she'd gained. The prestige. Her work.

For a moment, she feared she had degenerated to the wallowing mess of a teenager she'd once been in the years after ...

She hovered on the precipice of complete mental breakdown for a few seconds more before she was able to pull her panic back a fraction. Several more seconds saw the panic pulled back by half. Five minutes later, she was frazzled, but back to as close as she would ever get to "normal."

She rose to her feet unsteadily, and then once she was sure she wouldn't collapse with her first step, launched herself at her pants. She pulled them on with jerky movements, her harried breaths echoing around the room.

Once her armor of ugliness was in place, she allowed herself a deep breath.

"You're okay," she told herself, the words coming to her from the hidden place of daily repetition and long-term memory. "You depend on no one. You are your own person. Just make it through today." Her voice cracked.

The words didn't have the same effect they usually had, and she stared at the bed with longing.

Just one day, she thought fervently. *Just one day in bed. I won't let it get like it was in the beginning.* When she had spent several months without once leaving her room.

With a resigned sigh, Grace returned to bed, lay down, and pulled the covers over her head. Feeling as though she had taken a giant step back through years of progress, Grace wept.

...

Jayden leaned back against the pile of rubble and counted silently in his head, trying desperately to block out the sounds filling the hallway.

The defilers were…having *sex*.

The mouthy one and the blond one were in a room in the middle of the hall. The woman was moaning her mate's name over and over, and the blond one's accelerated breathing was so loud it sounded like continuous groans. But even more shockingly, similar sounds were coming from the room two doors closer to where Jayden stood where the blue-eyed one and the small, pregnant delicate one slept. What they could be doing when the female was so pregnant that *breathing* was uncomfortable, Jayden had no idea. And he tried hard not to imagine.

Jayden wanted to be disgusted with their obvious weakness for each other, but even his jaded mind had to acknowledge that what was happening between the couples was more than sex. Their emotions were rolling through the doors and slapping him upside the mind again and again. They were so in *love* with each other. Every thought that reached him was dripping with unbelievable pleasure and unbelievable care for the person they were with.

Jayden was about to fly apart at the seams.

He wanted his Temptation so badly he could taste it. He was standing as close to freedom and as far from the happy couples as he could get, trying to block out all of his senses. It was not working.

He buried his face in his hand and tried to breathe evenly and block out the sounds that were severely trying his control.

But then a sound reached him that was so distinct that he could not have blocked it out if he tried.

His Temptation wept.

Jayden straightened. His hearing narrowed, and for the first time, he was able to block the two couples out. He zoomed in on the door of his Temptation's room and cocked his head to the side.

Her ragged breathing flew down the hall and to his ears, slamming into him like a physical blow.

He staggered back, his wings brushing the rubble he had been leaning against, before surging forward. He flew down the hall before he could stop himself, and the next he was aware, he was pressed against her door. His forehead pressed against the metal. His hands were splayed at shoulder height. Every fiber of his body strained to be on the other side of the door.

Her thoughts were so dark that the cold seeped into his bones. He saw through her eyes the abuse of a human man. A man she had trusted.

Jayden yanked himself from her mind like he had been branded by what he found. His rapid breathing echoed through the hallway, and as he looked down, he noticed his hands were shaking. He did not want to know more. Feared what would have happened if he had stayed inside her mind to find out any more details. Feared what would happen with what little he had just learned.

He stumbled back until his back met the wall. Someone had hurt her. Hurt his Temptation. She hurt still. And he knew nothing about helping her. Knew instinctively that if he tried, it would only make things worse.

Something he had read in the mouthy one's mind filtered to the forefront of his thoughts. *She* had been hurt. Was now strong.

Jayden knew it was a bad idea before he even started walking toward the room that housed the mouthy one and her mate, but he could not stop himself. *Someone* needed to help his Temptation.

He hesitated for only a second before knocking twice on the door. The passionate sounds within abruptly stalled. The bed creaked, and then the door was thrown open.

The blond one glowered at Jayden from the doorway. The human was completely naked and, Jayden noticed right before immediately jerking his eyes to the ceiling, blatantly aroused. "What," the defiler growled.

"Jericho," the mouthy one whispered low enough she probably thought Jayden would not hear. "Win him over."

Jayden sighed and forced himself to look into the room past the blond one's shoulder. The mouthy one lay in bed, a sheet held up to her chin, her eyes curious. "She cries," Jayden said, appalled at the hopeless quality to his voice. "And I do not know what—"

Luckily, he did not have to say anymore. The woman leapt from the bed and began jerking on clothes, wrenching a curse from her mate who closed the door slightly and looked at Jayden with even more hate than the angel thought possible. "Don't you dare look at her," the blond one said.

Jayden was not remotely interested in seeing this man's mate bare, but Jayden did not respond. Moments later, the woman edged past her man, kissing him quickly on the cheek, and hustled down the hall to his Temptation's room.

"Grace?" the woman asked through the door. When there was no answer, she simply opened the door and went in.

Jayden was so focused on her actions that the brush along his forearm startled him into a defensive position. He jerked his eyes back to the blond one just in time to watch the man drop his hand from Jayden's skin. Jayden felt his eyes narrow, and immediately, he sent probes into the man's mind, trying to prepare for an attack of some kind.

He touched Jayden to use the gift of the Tree of the Knowledge of Good and Evil on him. What was more, the man was apparently shocked that he received both a *good* and an *evil* reading from the Knowledge.

Jayden was shocked, too. Angels were not regularly exposed to the Knowledge, but he could not imagine that they would be *either* good or evil. Angels just were.

The blond one looked at Jayden with a curious mix of lessening anger and increasing intrigue, and then said, "Dahlia will take care of her, angel. Don't you worry."

Jayden threw his shoulders back and glared. "I worry about nothing, human. You would do well to remember that." Jayden stalked back down the hall and took up his station against the rubble again, studiously preventing himself from reaching out toward the minds in the room at the end of the hall to see if his Temptation's hurt was abating at all.

Chapter Seven

When Grace woke the next morning, still exhausted from a night of crying, her first coherent thought was of a pleasant warmth at her back.

The *warmth* made her stiffen, but the *pleasant* delayed any immediate leap from bed. She felt her brow furrow as she tried to get her bearings, and then she realized that someone was in the bed with her.

Before panic could set in, Grace remembered that it was Dahlia. The woman had come to her rescue the night before and then sat with her all through the night, simply making sure Grace was not alone while she cried. It was the first time in her life someone had done such a thing for Grace.

Moving so slowly it could barely be called moving at all, Grace turned from her side to her back and looked at Dahlia. The woman was sitting on an impossibly small span of mattress. Her head was tossed far back, but Grace could still see her sleep-closed eyes and her slightly slack mouth. Dahlia's back was propped against the headboard; her left hand rested on her slight baby bump, and her right hand rested on Grace's shoulder.

Grace sucked in a breath and braced for the pain human touch always brought.

Nothing.

It didn't hurt. Grace stared at the slim, brown hand for what seemed like an eternity before she admitted that, not only didn't the touch hurt, but Grace didn't necessarily *mind* it.

The revelation was earth shattering.

Dahlia's hand was warm, and comforting. Grace frowned, but still didn't move away. Perhaps the fruit had healed more than just her physical wounds?

The door to her room was wide open, so nothing impeded the cacophonous sound of a door flinging open down the hall. Dahlia jerked awake, and Grace sat up so quickly she felt dizzy.

"Help," a man's distressed voice yelled out. "We need help!"

Grace and Dahlia swung into the hall, one right after the other and saw a very panicked Eli Johnson standing in the hallway. "Eli?" Dahlia asked in a voice still smothered by sleep.

Three doors down, another door opened as Jericho rushed into the hall. "What's wrong?" he asked.

"Abilene's water broke." Eli's blue eyes rolled around in panic. "I think she's in labor."

Grace felt her mouth drop open, and as one, all three of them ran down the hallway toward the rapidly unraveling Eli. Jericho and Dahlia asked questions simultaneously, ducking into the room and rushing to Abilene's side.

Grace stopped at the doorway.

Abilene looked fine. More than fine, actually. She was propped up against the headboard quietly reading a book.

Jericho and Dahlia immediately calmed as well. Dahlia walked to Abilene's side and began a quiet conversation with her while Jericho diverted to Eli to try to calm him—he was the only one in distress in the room.

Grace heard a noise to her left, and turned her head. The angel was at his usual post: leaning up against the rubble of the cave-in. He wasn't looking at her, though something told Grace she had his full attention. It didn't appear as though he had moved even one of his beautiful feathers since Eli's announcement, but his body was thrumming with tension. His wings were cocked and ready for flight, and the feathers were shimmering.

He must have felt her eyes on him, because he lifted his head and looked at her. His eyes were so beautiful. Grace felt herself flinch as pain worse than any she had felt so far rocketed through her body.

The angel's eyes narrowed, and his mouth opened as though he were going to speak.

She quickly dragged her gaze from the angel and back into Abilene's room, needing to distract herself from the pain before she did something foolish. Jericho had gotten Eli to calm a bit, and Dahlia was still talking to Abilene. Dahlia moved to one of the many monitors lining Abilene's bed and read the feed to her.

"Wait," Abilene said, straightening in her bed. "What?"

Dahlia repeated the feed.

The only piece of equipment Grace recognized, the heart monitor, began to speed up.

"That can't be right," Abilene said, shaking her head. Abilene reached a hand beneath the blankets as the room turned deadly quiet. The look of concentration on her angelic face disintegrated into absolute horror. "Oh, God, I feel like I'm ten centimeters already."

Eli walked to her side and grabbed her hand. "Um, isn't that a good thing, baby?"

Abilene swallowed a huge gulp of air, her ringlets bouncing vigorously as she shook her head. "But there's no pain!" Her voice ended on a hysterical note. "Oh my God, there's something wrong."

Grace's heart plummeted, and she stepped forward as everyone in the room began to lose their cool. They were severely unprepared for a complicated delivery.

Grace jumped as the angel's voice sounded from right beside her. "Of course there is no pain, human," he said softly.

Even though his voice had been quiet, everyone stopped mid-word and turned to him. He *tsk*'ed in annoyance. "She has eaten of the Tree of Eternal Life," the angel said shortly and with an air that led Grace to believe that he thought he had just explained everything. If the others' expressions were any indication, they were still just as confused as she was.

With a sigh, the angel continued, "Her delivery will be entirely painless. Excruciating labor is a curse of the Tree of Knowledge. That one," he nodded unceremoniously at Dahlia, "will have a *very* difficult time. But you, little human," he turned to Abilene, "will feel nothing."

Very slowly, they all turned to look at Dahlia. Grace watched as the blood drained from her face, an ashen look spreading beneath her warm caramel skin. "E-excuse me?" Dahlia asked.

The angel frowned. "I sincerely believe you would not want to know details." The statement was delivered without any inflection. Without any emotion. But the words were so grave a chill skittered up Grace's spine.

Dahlia attempted a laugh, but it came out forced. "I've gone through labor before, angel. I know it's no picnic."

The angel shook his head. "Not like this, you have not."

Dahlia took a step back. Her eyes grew wide, and she nodded once. Then her knees failed her. Jericho caught her just before she hit the floor. "Shit! Sweetheart?" When Dahlia gave no response, he hauled her up into his arms and cradled her against his chest. With a venomous glare at the angel, he stalked forward. "What the *hell* is wrong with you, angel!" Then, just as quickly, his face fell into utter hopelessness. "Will she…she won't…*die*, will she?"

They all waited impatiently for the angel to answer, and his facial expression did not put Grace at ease. "She has eaten of the Tree of Eternal Life. In the end, the birth of her child will not be what ends her."

Which, Grace noticed, was not a *no*. And, once again, Grace was reminded of this angel's endgame: their deaths.

Jericho's eyes turned bleak, and he kissed his unconscious wife on the forehead. Grace moved aside as Jericho carried Dahlia out while mumbling nonsense into her hair. His deep voice cut off abruptly as he closed them into their room. Grace looked back to Abilene, who had a hand covering her mouth, a look of horror painting her features. Eli was whispering in her ear, obviously trying to calm her, but the heart monitor was still beeping extraordinarily fast.

Grace glared at the angel. "Well done, you complete ass," she hissed. Profanity was usually beneath her—she had so many more refined ways of using words to cut someone to the quick—but nothing seemed to embody this situation better.

The angel's eyes flared as though he was surprised at Grace's rancor, and then he looked at the frantic couple across the room and heaved a resigned sigh.

With slow steps, the angel made his way toward Abilene. "Human, you must calm. You are not in danger, and your anxiousness is bad for the child."

Abilene's eyes snapped in his direction, a very clear expression of *you've gotta be kidding me* on her face. "Are you completely deranged?" she asked him in a loud voice. "Who says that to a pregnant woman? Who?"

"Baby, please—" Eli tried to pull her close to him, to wrap his arms around her.

"No! This is bullshit! He's holding us hostage. I'm about to give birth in captivity. And he goes around saying something doom and gloom every five seconds. I've had it!" Abilene's face turned red.

An alarm started blaring from one of the monitors.

• • •

Initially, he had come over here only to lesson some of his Temptation's anger; however, Jayden felt a genuine and rare flare of concern as a monitor for the baby's heartbeat began to blare in warning. The mother's anxiety was affecting the health of the innocent. The small woman reached beneath the blankets again, and a second later shrieked, "I'm crowning!"

The blue-eyed one swayed on his feet. "Oh, God, the baby's coming." He turned toward Jayden's Temptation with wide eyes. "What the hell am *I* supposed to do? I don't know anything about this!"

And then, against all reason or anything Jayden ever would have expected, his Temptation turned her eyes upon *him*. The silent plea in their depths shot straight through Jayden's spine. Jayden clenched his jaw and squeezed his eyes shut. This went against his instinct. His orders were to *end* these people, not to help them.

But the innocent was in danger. And the innocent was the priority.

"There is very little you have to do," Jayden said to the man quietly. "Her body does the work. You only need to catch your daughter." He walked forward slowly, mentally preparing himself for what he was about to do. "Little human," he said as kindly as possible to the small, frightened woman in the bed.

Her wide, terror-filled eyes turned on him. The alarm continued to sound.

"I know you are frightened, but you must calm. Remember yourself."

With his eyes, Jayden urged the blue-eyed one to take her hand, and once he did, Jayden felt the delicate one mentally take the reins of her panic and try to pull them back. "Yes, good," he coached her softly.

After a few moments, the alarm faltered and then fell silent. Jayden allowed himself to relax. He placed his hand on the blue-eyed one's shoulder and urged him to the end of the bed. "Tell him what to do," Jayden told the delicate one. "He is strong for his family. He will take care of you."

Without another word, Jayden turned from the bed, strode past his Temptation where she gaped at him with a wide-open mouth, and took up residence leaning against the wall right outside the room.

Less than a minute later, the indignant cry of a newborn babe filled the air. Though he told himself not to look—that *life* was none of his concern—Jayden could not stop himself from peeking into the room.

The blue-eyed one held an infant so tiny it barely filled his palms. The baby was warm and wiggly and perfectly formed. She had a head full of ebony ringlets, and she gazed upon her father with wide, blue eyes. Jayden's heart swelled as the infant's innocence flooded his body like a warm, consuming fire.

This was every angel's favorite part of humanity—the perfect, innocent beginning. He felt his cheeks burn and realized he was smiling. This new life—she was beautiful. The infant scowled at Jayden over her father's shoulder and her tiny, perfect face twisted as she screamed with all the power her small lungs could give her. The infant's feelings poured out of her: she wanted—no, *needed*— the woman in the bed. Loved her mother.

The feelings were so pure, so perfect, not even the blue-eyed one was confused about what she needed. He walked quickly to his mate's bedside and placed the baby on her mother's chest. The delicate one gasped and cuddled her child close to her breast. The defilers' intense, unconditional love for the baby permeated the room, strong and unforgiving, and Jayden was momentarily humbled by the selflessness of the humans' feelings.

The blue-eyed one climbed into bed with his family and wrapped his arms around the woman and child. "Oh, God, she's so beautiful," he said reverently, brushing a palm over the baby's head and pressing a kiss to his mate's cheek. "A girl," he whispered. "I was secretly hoping for a girl."

"So," the delicate one said, "Genesis it is."

The blue-eyed one nodded and pulled his family close.

Jayden watched all of this without a word. All he could think of was that he was going to soon take this child's—*Genesis's*—parents from her. Introduce pain into Genesis's young life. Return beautiful, guiltless love with pain.

It did not settle well within his heart.

He felt warmth at his side and turned his head. His Temptation stood beside him. "Thank you," she whispered, gifting him with the smallest and shyest of smiles.

Jayden felt it down to the tips of his toes. He tore his eyes from her and looked again at Genesis. The first life he had ever started rather than ended. And then a thought so shocking it had him stumbling backward flashed through his mind: *Do I have to kill them?*

The Compulsion rioted within him, and Jayden used all of his strength to push it back down again.

Weariness weighed Jayden down. Of course he had to. In the end, it mattered not whether he wanted to. It *would* happen. Doubting himself now would only bring on the Compulsion quickly.

He forced his eyes from the beautiful family and walked away.

Chapter Eight

The next morning, Jayden was in his usual place by the cave-in, but a very unusual aura of worry crowded his thoughts.

He could not shake a concern that the humans were going to run out of food.

Jayden had not once checked the supplies since packing the defilers into this wing of the facility—he hadn't cared if they lived longer or died sooner. But now, with an infant in their numbers, it seemed unnecessarily cruel to have such a cavalier attitude toward the humans' survival. After all, the infant they named Genesis was also human, and she did *not* deserve to suffer.

The worry continued to dig into Jayden's thoughts. With an exasperated sigh, Jayden pushed off of the rubble and stalked down the hallway toward the supply closet to check on the number of MREs. Hopefully no one would see him in this expression of caring, however little it might be.

Jayden wrenched open the supply closet, quickly scanned the contents, and frowned. No, they did not have nearly enough supplies for five grown adults and a growing child for seven months.

Jayden was running figures in his head when another steady stream of worry filtered through Jayden's mind. For a moment, he was completely confused. Was he truly worrying about yet another problem? Heaven above, he was going completely soft!

It took him only a moment more to realize the second stream of thoughts was not *his*. They were his Temptation's. They felt so important to him, so close to what he should be paying heed to, that he had mistaken them for his own thoughts.

He raised a hand and massaged his furrowed brow. With a steeling breath, he relaxed his mental guard and allowed his Temptation's thoughts to flood him fully.

The sheer volume of her anxiety almost bowled him over. He had to take a stumbling step back. Her complete lack of options for distraction was driving her toward the edge of what she could handle mentally. Always before, she had her work to distract her. God, the pain hurt so badly. She needed to be busy. *Pain*. Now she had nothing. Was trapped in a hallway with two happy couples and her worst nightmare. Why was this happening to her? She had nothing. No laptop. No research. *PAIN*. No projects. Nothing. *Nothing. NOTHING!*

Jayden jerked himself out of her thoughts with a gasp. A longing reared its head within him. The desire to ease her hurt—to fix her problem—was so overwhelming, Jayden could not ignore it.

Without thought, he began to rationalize taking action. He *had* just been pondering how it did not seem just to imprison them without creature comforts. Granted, *food* was not so much a comfort as a necessity, but—

Jayden stared down the hallway at the pile of rubble blocking the exit. It would take seconds—perhaps a minute—to return to the main room and retrieve some of his Temptation's items.

He allowed his senses to probe the other defiler's rooms. They were occupied the same way they were always occupied when the doors were closed. This time, however, the realization that they were all making love left him with a heavy feeling of want rather than disgust.

Jayden forcefully shoved that line of thought from his mind, and in its wake laid a decision. Was he really going to do this? Seek to make her stay with him more comfortable?

He took three steps toward the exit before he realized there had never really been a decision to make at all.

• • •

The breathing exercises weren't working! Grace could hear her breaths echoing throughout the sparse room, and at the rate that she was pacing back and forth, it wasn't only from hyperventilation. She was going to start wearing a literal path in the floor if she didn't get a hold of herself.

Another bolt of pain shot up her spine, and Grace gritted her teeth and walked faster. It didn't work. She was unable to prevent a whimper, no matter how fast she paced. The pain was so much worse today. It was the third day since she had Impulse-paired. She'd made it longer without release than any of the other two couples made it during the first few days of their relationships—and that thought, which had been her first upon waking today, no longer gave her any comfort.

Grace groaned as the pain continued and rubbed fingers over her temples, trying to hold back the raging migraine perched in the wings. "I need to work!" she shouted to the empty room.

Immediate chagrin rushed in. Had she seriously just screamed in an empty room like a toddler?

The thoughts of her laptop and research just feet away, but as inaccessible as though they were miles away were torturing her.

She had just spun on her heel to make another pass in front of the door for perhaps the ten thousandth time when a sharp knock sounded.

She jerked it open and was met with a rather timid-looking angel. Before she could stop herself, she looked at his wings where they peeked over his broad shoulders.

Why? Why did *he* get to disappear?

She could feel the ferocity of her scowl as she dragged her eyes from his wings to his face and was marginally pleased when the angel leaned away from her slightly. Oh, she was itching for a fight, and he was the perfect culprit. "*What?*" she growled, hands on hips.

His eyes flicked away from hers and danced around without landing on anything. In someone else, Grace would call the behavior *nervousness*.

"I thought…perhaps…" The angel's chest rose and fell with a quick huff, and he stared at the ceiling momentarily, dismay and annoyance flaring across his face. He met her eyes again and drew his hands from behind his back. "Here," he said unceremoniously, thrusting a battered brown bag at her.

Grace stared at it for several seconds before she recognized it as her beat-up leather satchel. She could see the corner of her laptop peeking through the edge of the flap. "Is that what I think it is?"

"Well…yes. I, uh, thought you might need. Well—" He broke off and looked at the floor again. He wiggled the satchel where it still hovered between them.

Grace snatched it from his fingers, careful not to touch him, and pulled it to her chest. She could see notes peeking from the back pocket—notes that had been on her desk. He'd seen them and made sure to put them in the bag for her.

The gesture made her irrationally angry. "You think this what, makes us okay now or something?" she spat at him.

His head shot up and his eyes widened. "No, I—"

"Shut up," she snapped. "God, you're all the same!" And even though she hated him in that second, she couldn't prevent herself from looking at his body. His robe had mended itself from the gunshot wound he received days ago, and the blood had vanished from its fabric. It lay on his body like the finest silk. His wide chest filled it out beautifully, and she discovered herself licking her lip. She forced herself to sneer at a splash of blood that marred the flawless patch of skin at the base of his neck where his robe did not reach. If she didn't go on the offense, and soon, she would throw herself at him. That patch of skin would be her undoing. The Impulse pain flared hotly, and she turned the groan of pain into a stinging retort. "Don't you ever bathe?" she threw into his face. She scowled at him and spun around.

With that, she slammed the door in his face.

And immediately felt like shit. She looked down at the bag she still clutched to her chest and noticed that he'd even tucked her favorite pen in with the notes. The pain flared again along with the realization that she'd been a class-A bitch.

Did he deserve it? Oh, yeah. But "winning him over," the group's current brilliant plan for escape, might have just been shot to hell. With a weary sigh, she gently set her satchel down on the bed and walked to the door, not quite sure she was really getting ready to apologize to the psycho who was holding her captive.

When she opened the door this time, it was with dread. But the hallway was empty. Grace looked right and left and didn't see him. The door of the room next to hers was standing open, however, and she figured he'd gone in there to pout. Or whatever it was angels did when chubby redheads ripped them a new one. Her feet dragged as she forced herself to walk into the adjacent room, an apology ready to trip off of her tongue as soon as she saw him so she could get this over with.

She spun into the room. "Angel, I'm s—" She stumbled to a stop.

The angel's hand paused where it was dribbling water from the running sink over his bare pectoral. Over his bare *everything*. The angel's robe lay in a puddle on the floor at his feet. He was standing by the hand-washing sink in the corner and giving himself a whore's bath, except looking at him made *Grace* want to be the whore.

Everywhere her eyes caressed was covered with beautiful, burnt-sugar skin. His muscles flickered beneath her stare. His chest glistened where he had been trickling water over the long-gone wound. Her eyes followed a droplet as it ran between his pecs and picked up speed as it bounded down the center division of his abs. The droplet was halted by his belly button, but Grace's eyes didn't stop. She heard herself make a noise of complete and utter *want* as she allowed herself to look at the evidence that this angel was very much a *male*.

No sooner had she looked and realized that she was looking at the most beautiful thing she had ever seen than the pain from the Impulse crashed through her. It was so intense, it made her sag against the doorframe and bite her lip hard enough to draw blood. With a moan, she tore around the corner and fled to her room.

Pain, worse than any she'd felt thus far, shot through her body, throwing her onto her bed. Her body arched. Her head thrashed on the pillow. Her toes curled.

Oh, she *needed*.

Images of the angel flew behind her closed eyes. The way he moved. The way he looked at her.

On its own, her hand began to move. Her fingers dug under the waistband of her scrubs. Quickly slipped between her panties and her skin. Her fingers were so warm; they seemed to burn where they touched.

A moan wrenched from Grace's lips, and she bit her bottom lip to keep it from happening again.

She started breathing quickly. Her mind replaced her own hand with the big, blunt fingers of the angel. It was no longer she who touched herself. It was *him*.

Grace felt a rush of warmth between her thighs. Her knees fell open in response. Her fingers tunneled further, sifting through the curls at the apex of her thighs. As soon as her fingertips encountered the moisture thoughts of the angel had wrung from her body, Grace groaned.

Oh, *God*, she was aroused.

She had never been aroused in her life. It was the most uncomfortable feeling she had encountered. Worse than pain. Worse than fear.

More demanding than them both combined.

"*Angel*," she whispered as her finger moved further, sliding through her slick folds to the indentation where she ached the most.

Her heart was beating nearly out of her chest as she tentatively pushed her index finger into her body.

She was so warm. So wet. The discovery brought on another rush of heat, and her body began to throb uncontrollably just a scant inch above where her fingers rested.

Her back arched again, and her fingers shot up. Drenched with her own desire, they passed over the throbbing bundle of nerves at the top of her sex. As soon as her index finger passed over the spot, Grace cried out.

She brought her left hand up to her mouth, covering it desperately as another cry tore from her body. Her finger began to move.

• • •

Jayden stared dumbly at the doorframe that mere moments ago had held his Temptation, and wondered what in the world had just happened. He bent to sweep his robe up and over his head, and walked out into the hallway and to the closed door of her room. He paused then. What was he supposed to do now? Knock? Again? That did not go so well last time.

He was contemplating this problem when her pleasure reached him, nearly bowling him over.

She was experiencing the greatest physical pleasure she had ever known. She was panting with it. Her body was dripping with it.

She moaned, and Jayden heard himself echo it heartily, shifting himself so he was pressed completely against the door from chest to knee. Her thoughts were what reached him next.

She was thinking…of *him*. She was thinking of his body and touching her own. Picturing his chest. She longed to dig her fingernails in it. To rest her head upon it.

The ache in his belly Jayden had been studiously ignoring since first seeing his Temptation became more pronounced. It was more intense, and gaining in intensity every second. It *hurt*. He moaned softly. And then, pressure traveled down from his navel. His shaft moved against his leg, filling. Rising. It pressed against the cold metal door through the fabric of his robe. He drew back in shock.

He was…*aroused*.

He had never once, in all his millennia of existence, been aroused. Oh, he had seen such a condition in human men, and the behavior—mostly bad—it incited. But now, he understood why. The ache in his belly increased.

With a groan, he realized he would do almost anything to relieve it.

His Temptation's thoughts switched from his chest to his eyes. She loved them. Loved the color. Pictured them in her mind.

His stomach trembled. His knees weakened. He groaned so hard, his throat hurt. His arousal throbbed, and, oh, how he ached to touch it. To wrap his hand around it and picture her beautiful gray eyes as she pictured his.

She cried out as waves of ecstasy poured throughout her body.

Jayden fisted his hands at his side and pressed his forehead against the door, fighting for air and for control.

Her physical pain was gone, but Jayden knew the moment it was replaced with emotional pain. Her fear and frustration was an acrid taste on his tongue. Her thoughts faltered and fell from pleasure to past. To a man she once thought she could desire. The first man who ever expressed a desire for her. The man who had… *God in heaven.*

The man who had *raped* her. Rage—so powerful, so violent—flooded him.

And then her sobs penetrated the haze once more, and Jayden erupted.

With a roar, he pivoted on his feet. He was seeing red. He launched himself at the wall directly across from her door and pounded into it with both fists, his knuckles breaking through the sheetrock clear to the other side. He threw his head back and *yelled* with all of his might to the ceiling.

Behind him, her door clicked and squeaked as she slowly opened it.

He felt his sword, strapped to his back, send off waves of heat. He turned toward her. She stood so small and so helpless in the doorway. Her eyes were red-rimmed and flooded with tears, but the sorrow was no longer in them. Instead, she was looking at him with a blend of curiosity and fear.

"Who is he?" Jayden asked darkly.

She gasped and stepped back. "W-what do you—"

"The human," he cut her off. "The human who touched what is mine. Who. Is. He."

Fire filled her eyes and she stepped out into the hallway. "Yours?" she snarled at him. "Who the *hell* do you think you are? I belong to *no one!*" Quick as lightning, her tiny fist flared out and punched him in the chest.

Jayden blinked, his rage at this unforeseen enemy evaporating in the absurdity of what she had just done.

"Ow, son of a *bitch!*" she yelled, shaking her hand in the air.

Jayden clicked his tongue and snatched her hand from the air to cradle in his. Her knuckles were already swollen and turning a dark shade of purple. Even knowing that her body would heal itself quickly, the sight hurt him far more than her ineffectual punch. "Temptation, that was unwise," he murmured, passing a thumb over her knuckles.

She stopped moving. Stopped breathing.

He looked at her face and was startled by her wide gray eyes. She looked as though she hovered between panic and more panic.

He clicked his tongue again. "Does it hurt so badly?"

She shook her head slowly. "It…doesn't hurt…at *all*."

She sounded baffled and her eyes fell to where he held her hands. Suddenly, their touch felt anything but impersonal, and Jayden dropped her hand as quickly as he could. What had he been doing, touching her?

She looked away, but not so quickly that Jayden did not see something that looked like disappointment flash across her face. Her thoughts were a riotous jumble that mirrored Jayden's own. She desperately wanted to be alone.

She arrived at the one thing she could vocalize to end their conversation, though her thoughts were embarrassed that she would say something so stupid. "Um," she whispered to the ground nevertheless, "thank you for my bag."

Without another word, she walked into her room and shut the door.

Chapter Nine

Jayden lay on the bed in the room next to hers for the rest of the night staring at the ceiling. He could not sleep. Angels never slept. In fact, if an Angel *did* sleep, his Fall was near. It was an indication that all was lost. So, Jayden lay in bed *thinking*.

This was why it was imperative for the sons of God to stay away from their Temptations.

Thinking? About his mission?

Never happened. Not until he had witnessed the birth of a child. Not until he had tried to make the life of his Temptation easier. Not until he *touched* her.

Hours passed like seconds, and Jayden heard the humans begin to stir from their sleep. Heard Genesis cry. Heard Genesis's mother and father leap to attend to her needs.

The limited supplies in the closet flitted through his mind again, and Jayden groaned. He still had not fully thought of a solution.

Jayden frowned and looked above him at the window over the bed. The sun was rising. He sat up slowly, giving himself some more time to think, before leaving the bed and moving to the door. He leaned out into the hall.

The humans were gathering for their morning meal—a procedure they had fallen into rather quickly. They had turned one of the medical wing rooms into a mess hall of sorts. Jayden would find them there.

He treaded silently down the hallway, paused at the door, took a deep breath, and walked in. The five adults in the room immediately stopped cooing at Genesis to stare at him. Jayden realized he had never once joined them for a meal. Preferring to keep his much-needed distance, he spent most of his time guarding the cave-in site.

He ignored their gaping as much as possible and took the only empty chair around the table. That there was an empty chair was not missed by him. The humans left a place for him in this part of their daily routine.

Genesis made some unidentifiable noise between a grunt and a cry from the arms of her mother, not content to share attention with a surly angel, and like magic, all the adults returned their eyes to her, cooing and in general making great fools of themselves to please her.

He braced himself and then spared a quick glance at his Temptation. Like he expected, the sight of her was like a fist to his gut. The morning light streaming through the window bounced off of her copper curls.

But, then he noticed the tight lines of her face. The way she could not really look at anything, adorable infant included, for too many seconds together. Her hands were fisted in her lap, and he was certain she was biting the inside of her cheek.

Jayden frowned. She had peaked yesterday. He knew this intimately. He had been outside of her door to witness it—it was something Jayden would never forget. He knew from the others' thoughts that this should be enough to keep the Impulse pain away. Why would she still be suffering?

Her misery was palpable. How was it that all the others were able to ignore it? It cut through him.

His attention snapped to the Genesis's parents. "You and you," he said, harsher than he intended.

Silence reigned again, and Genesis's mother and father turned their eyes upon him warily.

"Gather your belongings and prepare the child. You are leaving." The words took even Jayden by surprise, but he could not back out now. It was not the best solution to the supply problem, but it would work.

As Jayden looked at Genesis, he realized that he was relieved for her. Jayden would still hunt the two defilers down. Still kill them. But the Compulsion was proximity-based. Sending them away would buy the family months—possibly even years, if Jayden could get himself to focus on the three prisoners overseas—of precious time. Time Genesis would have with her parents. Time she needed.

He could not release them all. That would just speed up the process. He was barely able to hold back the inevitable now, and he was certain it was only because they were all here, under his control. He needed at least one of them nearby to delay the Compulsion. He doubted the blond one would leave his mouthy one, so he would keep them both. And his Temptation? Well, even considering sending her away was a moot point. Like all his brothers, once Jayden laid his eyes upon her, he would not be able to leave her side. The very thought of leaving her made him anxious. His only hope now was to resist further entanglement with her.

Genesis's parents turned to him in shock. "We're allowed to go?" Genesis' mother asked, the beginning of a smile crossing her face.

"Yes. Quickly." Before he changed his mind.

The woman seemed to hear his unspoken addendum, for she launched to her feet with the baby in her arms and left the room without another word. Genesis's father stayed behind only to say a quick, "Thank you," before he also left.

In the wake of their exit, the silence was oppressive. Jayden finally forced himself to meet his Temptation's eyes only to immediately wish he had not. She was staring at his wings blankly, shocking torment on her features.

He was also shocked when none of the remaining three asked *What about me?* or *Why them?* He had been mentally preparing for such questions, but when they did not arrive, Jayden knew not what to do. From the noises coming right next-door, it sounded as though the family would be ready to leave in no time at all. So, Jayden got up from the table and left the room, breathing a sigh once he reached the hallway and was no longer under his Temptation's scrutiny.

It was an easy task to remove a few boulders from the cave-in. Just enough for the adults to slip out one at a time, and easy enough for Jayden to guard in the meantime.

Just as he finished laying aside the last boulder, he turned to find the two humans ready to leave, Genesis in arms. Abilene smiled at him briefly, and then ducked through the exit with the baby.

As Eli moved to do the same, Jayden stopped him with a hand to his shoulder. The man stiffened and continued to stare forward. "Human, I—" Jayden forced himself to continue. "Anything you can do to discourage a rescue attempt—please. I do not know if I could stop myself from—"

Eli hesitated a second before looking Jayden in the eye. Those blue eyes stared for several moments before the man nodded curtly. "Thank you," he said again. Then he quickly followed his wife.

Relief and, again, the feeling of rightness settled over Jayden, even though by letting the two go, he was technically going against orders. How could going against his orders feel so right? He hissed as he realized he'd mentally called them all by their actual names. Unease settled in as Jayden quickly piled the rocks again, making sure no human could get in or out without his knowledge.

Then he returned to the room where they ate. It was disturbing how empty the wing felt now without the three humans. Without

Genesis. Jayden realized how much he had enjoyed the infant's presence, even if he never interacted with her.

When he passed through the doorway, he came to a stumbling stop. His Temptation was alone in the room. A quick use of his senses told him that the other couple was in their room. Making love. Again.

Jayden grimaced.

From the look on his Temptation's face, she knew what the other two were up to as well. For the briefest of moments, thoughts of the orgasm she had given herself yesterday passed through her mind, but just as quickly, her memories of the rape flashed.

It was the first time since their interlude yesterday that Jayden sensed her directions take that path, which was the longest break since he had first encountered her. He did not like that her thoughts returned there now.

He felt himself move forward. "No one is allowed to hurt you, you know."

Her head snapped in his direction, surprise at his presence flaring in her eyes. She had not known he was in the room.

The surprise quickly vanished to be replaced with pique. "No one except for you," she said tersely.

And just like that, all the relief releasing the three humans brought vanished, to be replaced with something that felt alarmingly like...*fear*.

He *was* going to hurt her. He could not part from her, could not even think about it, and so she would be with him when the Compulsion struck.

Jayden quickly thrust those thoughts from his mind. He would go mad if he allowed himself to think on them for long. He pointedly ignored her last statement and approached the table where he sat to her right.

She eyed him warily from the corner of her eyes, but the flare of lust did not miss his notice. He closed his eyes and breathed deeply of her skin. Being close to her calmed the majority of his anxiety, and he was grateful.

Riding on the heels of that feeling came these words: "You can defend yourself from such a thing in the future, Temptation."

She stared at him dumbly for several seconds, and then scoffed. She raised one brow and gestured to her body with one hand. "Oh, yeah. I'm a regular ninja."

He did not understand what she meant, but something told him she was insulting herself. He frowned.

When he did not speak again, she went on. "Don't worry. I've done everything I can to make sure no one wants me that way ever again. I mean," she gestured at herself again, "look at me. I'm smaller than I used to be, but this is still bigger than men want."

Heat spiked behind Jayden's heart. First, if anyone else said this about her, he would kill them. The fact that she said it about herself drove him to the brink of an outburst. Second, he did not want her thinking about what other men wanted at all, only what *he* wanted.

Jealousy and rage.

Jayden realized he had been feeling a flurry of emotions this day, something that he could not allow to happen and keep the Compulsion at bay. He forced himself to calm. "You will not talk about yourself in such a manner," he said smoothly, earning a disbelieving look from his Temptation. "Besides, you are vastly mistaken if you think your appearance would detract anyone from wanting you." He allowed how much he wanted her to come to the forefront for a moment, looking at her with a heated glare.

She colored beneath his scrutiny and looked away. Confusion passed through her mind. She truly did not realize her allure.

Unbelievable. Jayden shot up from the table and strode to the door, desperately needing a distraction. Desperately needing to distract *her*. The work he had brought her only yesterday was clearly not diverting her enough. When he turned around to look at her, she was still staring at the table. "Come," he said shortly.

She looked at him. Pink stained her cheeks as she remembered what it felt like to do just that only hours ago. Her eyes cast down to the floor.

Jayden swallowed past a star-sized lump in his throat. "Come," he couldn't prevent himself from repeating, his voice now impossibly deep and rough.

"Where?" she snapped, her eyes jerking back to his censoriously. Her brow furrowed, and her eyebrows crashed down.

She knew he repeated it to get a rise out of her, and she was upset with him, he realized. And what was worse, she was *beautiful* when she was upset with him. Jayden forced his mind to other things. "We are going to fight."

Her eyes widened. "What?"

"We are going to fight. Practice," he gestured to the hall. "I will teach you how to defend yourself, and then you will no longer have to worry."

She laughed without humor. "You've gotta be kidding me. If I wanted to learn self-defense to protect myself, I would have taken a freakin' karate class years ago. I protect myself in other ways."

Jayden crossed his arms. "These other ways. They have worked for you? You are not, for example, currently imprisoned?"

It was a low blow, and they both knew it. Her eyes narrowed, and her mouth opened. No doubt to deliver a terrible set-down of some sort.

A loud, feminine moan sounded from the room next door. His Temptation blushed and looked at the ground again.

"Do you have anything else you would rather be doing right now?" Jayden asked, shocked by the innuendo in his tone. He had not meant the question to come out so…naughty.

Her eyes snapped to his, and he saw longing flare there briefly. Her thoughts returned to her pleasure, this time replacing her own touch with his. *His* fingers caressing her body. *His* touch bringing her to completion.

Jayden sucked in a breath. He turned quickly and left the room. She either would join him out here or she would not, but if he stayed in the small room with her one moment more, he would not be responsible for his actions.

Several seconds later, she stepped timidly into the hallway. "Are you serious about this?" she asked softly.

"I am always serious."

Her doubt lingered heavily in the air.

He would need to move slowly. Help her gain confidence. The truth was, she was much more capable than she guessed herself to be. He turned and walked to the end of the hallway, then pivoted back to face her. "Stand here," he said, pointing to a spot two feet in front of him.

She moved slowly forward, not yet meeting his eyes. She stopped where he pointed.

"Lesson one," he began, hoping she would look at him. "Hard to soft."

She finally did meet his eyes, but it was obvious she did not know what he meant. He held his arm out and pointed to his knuckles and then his elbow. "Hard—" then he patted his belly, "to soft."

She made a fist with the hand she had injured trying to punch him yesterday and looked down at it and then back at him disbelievingly.

"This is why you hurt yourself yesterday. Your hand is hard; my breastbone is hard. 'Tis not a good mix." She continued to stare at him mutely, her loosely formed fist before her. Jayden shifted uncomfortably beneath her stare. "Come on, think, Temptation," he said gently. "Where on my body am I soft?"

Her eyes roved down his front and then back to his eyes. He felt it like a caress.

"Nowhere?"

He made a noise that sounded oddly like a chuckle. Her widened eyes said she heard it. "No," he said before he could make a bigger fool of himself. "All men are soft here," he pointed to his eyes, "here," his throat, "here," his stomach, "and here," his groin.

Her eyes lingered on the last spot.

"Well, usually soft there," he amended quietly as he felt his body stir under her gaze. "Perhaps not when we are around you."

Her eyes flew to his face in wide shock at the same time he realized what he said. Dear Lord, was he…*flirting* with her?

And who said that to someone who had been through what she had been through? He quickly scanned her thoughts; preparing to apologize and try to ease the fear that such a statement would inevitably give her.

Instead, he discovered another flare of pain and lust. He swallowed hard as her eyes drifted from his face and back downward. "So try it," he blurted out over loud.

Victory. Her eyes returned to safe territory. "Try what?"

"Hit me."

She laughed. Several seconds later, "Oh, wait. You're serious?"

"I am always—"

"Serious." She rolled her eyes. "Yes, I've heard." She flashed him a brilliant smile that momentarily dazzled him, and then she moved much faster than he anticipated.

Her right fist flew forward and nailed him directly in his abdomen. Her strike had more power than he would have guessed, but it was still nothing. Nevertheless, he forced all of his air from his lungs with a loud *oof,* and doubled over, placing his hands on his knees. He held his huddled position for some time as he falsely struggled for breath before making a great show of cautiously returning to an upright position. He rubbed his stomach. "Good," he said with a wince.

"You know," she said, "that was actually kinda fun." Pure confidence flowed through her, no fear and no pain.

"Again?" he asked.

She nodded eagerly.

He reached forward and took her hand. As soon as their skin touched, her smile faded. She sucked in a surprised breath, and Jayden found his eyes coming to rest on the way her breasts moved with her gasp.

He forced his eyes back to her face and bent her fingers gently until she was making the peace sign that had grown so popular in the nineteen seventies. He brought her fingers to his face and made a slight jabbing motion toward his eyes. "Very effective move," he said in a hoarse voice. He let her hand fall back to her side.

She stared at him dumbfounded.

"Go on," he coached gently.

She tilted her head. "Stab you in the eyes?"

He nodded.

After a moment, she shrugged. Her strike this time was much less fierce out of fear of hurting him, but Jayden threw his hand up as a blade between his eyes to catch her fingers at their crux, stopping her fingertips just short of their mark.

She relaxed and smiled again.

"Excellent," he said. Her smile grew in response.

This time it was she who asked, "Again?"

Over the next few hours, Jayden showed her a variety of easy moves that boosted her confidence and had her gifting him with dozens of spontaneous smiles. By the time she yawned, Jayden was so worked up from casual contact with her body that he was more than ready to call it a night.

"Bed time, little one," Jayden said as her fatigue washed over him.

At his words, disappointment wafted through her mind along with anxiety that her thoughts would revert to fanaticizing about him without anything to distract her, but she nodded and turned toward her room. Just as she reached the door, Jayden stopped her.

"Tomorrow," he said, causing her to turn to him, "we will continue." He could give her this. With both of their minds and bodies otherwise occupied, they may have a fighting chance.

As soon as the words set in, she smiled brilliantly at him, joy and relief lighting up her gray eyes. "Okay," she said. "Good night, angel."

Jayden felt a burning in his cheeks. He smoothed his fingers over his lips only to discover he was smiling back at her.

Her eyes followed his fingers, and her thoughts skittered like butterflies, and he captured each one like it was a treasure. One thought she arrived at again and again: she used to *love* kissing. Wondered what it would feel like to kiss him.

Jayden felt his smile collapse beneath his fingers as need clenched tightly in his belly.

Her smile faded as well. She turned and went into her room and closed the door.

Jayden remained in the hall and stared at her closed door for several long minutes before going into his own room next door. He moved to the wall that separated them and pressed his hand to it at heart height.

Angel, she called him. With all of his being, he wished she would have said his name. But to do that, she would have to know it.

"Good night," Jayden whispered to the wall, "Grace."

Chapter Ten

Jayden was sitting outside his Temptation's room, huddled against the door, his head buried in his upraised knees while his Temptation's screams echoed down the hallway.

Physical pain, unlike any Jayden had witnessed in a human before, was tearing through his Temptation's body. Her thrashings rang clear through the door, as did the mouthy one's attempts to make things better.

The screams had started this morning. Jayden had been right outside her room when the torturous pain first tore through her. He had stumbled back against the wall, clutching his heart as it tried to beat out of his chest, while the defilers sprinted out of their room and into hers.

And things had only gotten worse.

The blond one eventually left, partly because Jayden's Temptation's screams distressed his male sensibilities, partly to think in quiet to try to determine what was happening to the writhing redhead.

Jayden mentally monitored the blond one's thoughts in a room at the end of the hall. The man was arriving at conclusions and discarding them left and right, but one idea was becoming prevalent, and it scared Jayden to within an inch of his life.

His idea was one Jayden had been considering as well since noticing his Temptation's self-given orgasm had not succeeded, and the time to act was fast approaching. Jayden could not stand much more of his Temptation's torture.

Jayden heard the blond one make his way down the hallway and braced himself. Slowly Jayden raised his head from his knees to look at him.

His Temptation let out a new wail that was so dripping with physical and emotional pain that Jayden watched the blond one wince and felt the same expression on his own face. Jayden closed his eyes tightly; his fingers dug into his knees as he struggled for control. When he opened his eyes again, the blond one's face had shifted slightly as he looked upon Jayden.

"Her pain *does* distress you," he said.

A thousand stinging retorts perched on the edge of Jayden's tongue. He wished he could deny it—they already guessed too much about his connection to her. But what he longed to say was, *More than you will ever know.*

Lord of the Most High, he *felt* her pain. Not the physical pain. No, Jayden never felt physical pain beyond the newly discovered discomfort of arousal. But his connection to this woman enabled him to feel her emotions and thoughts in a way keener than Jayden's ability allowed him with others. It was part of the reason Jayden had so much trouble resisting her.

And now, her emotional distress—her confusion over what was happening to her, her terror at the pain, her intense longing—was flowing through him as uncut and unfiltered as he had come to expect.

Instead of speaking, Jayden schooled his face into a mask—quite unsuccessfully he imagined—and looked at the blond one.

For the first time in days, the blond one softened toward Jayden. He folded his body into a sitting position across from Jayden in the hall, and said, "I knew you couldn't be all bad."

Jayden sneered, lashing out with, "Do not underestimate me, *human.*"

If the defiler felt the insult Jayden intended, he gave no indication, much to Jayden's annoyance. Instead, Jayden felt the man calmly collect his thoughts and prepare to speak.

And Jayden felt dread down to the tips of his toes. The man's theory flowed to him clearly, and now the words left the blond one's mouth before Jayden could stop them.

"I've been thinking about all our own experiences with the Impulse," the blond one began.

Jayden felt the wariness cross his face and cursed his weakness as the blond one tried to actually *calm* him.

"Hey, man," he said softly. "I know this isn't a comfortable topic, but you need to know."

"Why," Jayden blurted before he could stop himself. "Why do I need to know?"

The blond one continued, "We don't know exactly who you are or exactly why you're here, but we're not idiots, *angel*." Jayden straightened. Apparently his human-dig *had* hit a nerve. The blond continued. "You're on some kind of mission to kill those who have eaten from the Tree of Eternal Life, and we're all on the list." The man took a big breath and met Jayden's eyes. "Fine."

Jayden blinked. *Fine*? Well, that was a new reaction to facing imminent death. Jayden had to admit, his interest was piqued. "Fine?" he heard himself echo.

"Yes, fine. We're doomed. We're going to die. Whatever." Jayden frowned, but the man was not done. "But is part of your mission to torture living beings?"

Jayden's frown deepened.

"It seems to me that a God so concerned with protecting humanity that he would send an angel to ensure that protection would not look too kindly upon his *angels* prolonging agony in humans, even if those humans were destined to die." The blond one obviously saw that his words were having an effect, because he decided to tack on, "A kind, merciful, loving God would not want Grace to suffer, would he?"

Jayden ground his teeth. His Temptation *was* suffering. Jayden, of all living creatures, knew that intimately. To consign her to this suffering for seven more long, torturous months. Well, for one, *Jayden* would not survive it. "Speak," he ground out.

Triumph lit the blond one's eyes. "Okay, in all four of us," the man actually blushed, "all four of us—me and Dahlia, Eli and Abilene—we all experienced an orgasm within a short period of Impulse-pairing with our mates."

Jayden frowned and felt a flare of impatience. "So has she," he said with more venom than he intended.

"Yes," the blond one said. "But not with *you*. Her Impulse mate."

Jayden felt his heart drop. Yes, this was the idea he had been studiously avoiding since he first felt it flit through the man's mind.

The blond one continued, "Within hours, Eli had given Abilene an orgasm, and I gave Dahlia one after a day or so. What's the whole point of Impulse pain, man? Think about it."

Jayden did, and did not like the conclusion. He knew what the point had been for the *original* Impulse pair. The Most High had needed a way to bring the Impulse pair together. For the purpose of…*procreation*.

"Out of the question," Jayden said so softly, so dangerously that the blond one leaned back. Jayden would not *procreate* with his Temptation. That would be the end. That was how so many of his brothers had Fallen before. Lying with the daughters of men, creating *life* with the daughters of men—it was forbidden. Unforgivable. A sign of weakness.

And Jayden was not weak. "I will not lie with her."

A muscle ticked in the blond one's jaw. "You don't have to have sexual intercourse with her, angel," he said. "We didn't," he said gesturing to himself and then the direction of his mate. "Not for a while. Eli literally had to die first before Abilene would sleep with him." The corner of the blond one's mouth raised slightly in the shadow of a smile.

His Temptation screamed anew, her voice loud and long. And then, suddenly, her scream broke, her voice going hoarse, her sobs echoing out into the hallway.

Jayden's chest swelled, and he had to cover his mouth with his hand to keep from groaning. She had screamed until her voice *broke*.

The blond one's attempt at humor hung sourly between them, and the blond one's face grew grave. "You're not completely heartless. How can you let that," he gestured to the closed door beside Jayden, "continue if you can stop it?"

He could not. Jayden knew he could not. It was time to stop kidding himself. If the blond one had not come to him with this idea, put it into words, Jayden would have known it was the only way even without him.

But could he *touch* her? Lay his hands on her? Look upon her body and ever be the same again? She was his Temptation. His one and only vulnerability. His entire destiny depended upon him abstaining from her.

But her condition does not require consummation, his mind reminded him.

His Temptation's sobs grew in volume. And then, she did something that set in stone Jayden's next actions. Clearly and loudly enough so that all heard it, his Temptation cried out, "*Angel, please.*"

Before he even knew he moved, Jayden was on his feet, her call on him of greater importance than his own. Without a backward glance at the blond one who had jumped to his feet as well, Jayden shoved open the door to his Temptation's room. It flew in and bounced off of the wall with a crash, swinging back toward him. Jayden stopped it with his splayed hand.

The mouthy one who was standing over his Temptation's bed, jerked around to look at him with wide eyes.

"Get out," Jayden ordered.

Her eyes got wider. On the bed, his Temptation began to thrash. "Yes…*angel*," she moaned through dry, cracked lips.

"Get out!" Jayden bellowed.

"It's okay," the blond one said from behind Jayden. "Do what he says."

The woman moved toward the door, and Jayden stalked toward his Temptation, not paying any attention to the mouthy one as she began questioning her man, or the sound of the door as it was closed.

He stalled out at the foot of his Temptation's bed. Doubt plagued him. *Am I truly going to do this?*

He allowed himself to look upon his Temptation fully for the first time since storming into her space. She had quieted somewhat since Jayden entered the room. The sheets had been kicked completely from the bed, and, Jayden realized with a groan, she was completely naked. The touch of fabric on her skin must have been too much. Her hands were fisted in the sheets, and she twisted them restlessly. She bit into her bottom lip and looked at him, not really seeing him, from eyes burdened with the sheen of tears.

Oh, yes. He was going to do this.

He swallowed hard as his eyes roved over her body, starting with her toes. They were painted a soft, feminine pink color that made Jayden's stomach lurch. She tried so hard to hide any feminine part of her body, the past few days had only proven that, and yet, here were her pale, perfect feet, tipped with pink. With a trembling hand, Jayden reached for her, trailing his index finger over the top of her foot.

As soon as his finger touched her skin, all of her physical agony fled the room. Jayden literally felt it vanish.

His Temptation gasped in shock. Her eyes cleared. Sharpened slightly. "Angel?"

"Yes," he said, shocked at how raspy his voice was. How labored his breathing was. Knowing instinctively that removing his finger would bring the pain back. *Start small.* It would give them both more time to adjust. He trailed the finger down and lightly wrapped his fingers around her ankle.

Her skin burned his like the fires of hell. His knees grew weak. He knew he would embarrass himself unforgivably if he collapsed before her, and so he moved until he could sit on the edge of the bed next to where his hand touched her.

The bed dipped with his weight, and he looked upon where he held her. Her skin was so light and delicate. And soft. Jayden's hand looked large and dark in comparison, his deep brown skin contrasting with her pale complexion. The sight of his hand on her ankle, the feel of her flesh, sent a jolt of desire straight through Jayden's stomach, and his shaft filled instantly, swelling and standing straight up beneath his robe.

Jayden closed his eyes and begged for control. Though he knew very little about this intimate facet of humanity, his instincts were strong. He longed to cover her body with his. To bury his shaft within her. To cover her mouth with his lips as she gasped. He balanced on the edge of chaos.

And then her fear flitted through his mind.

She was afraid of what he was doing here. Alone with her. In a bedroom. He held still as her haunted memories of assault flew through her thoughts.

He squeezed her ankle softly. "I am not here to hurt you, Temptation," he whispered. He forced himself to look into her eyes, knowing that their gorgeous gray depths would try his control even more. Her eyes, framed with lush auburn lashes, were flooded with doubt. "I will not take you against your will. Will *never* take you," he said with feeling, reminding himself in the process.

He saw a different type of pain fill her eyes.

• • •

Will never *take you.*

He'd spoken with such feeling, such disgust. Grace was horrified to feel tears flooding eyes.

She disgusted him. Shame burned her cheeks as she reached for the sheet so she could cover her naked body. She jerked on it fitfully, but the angel's weight held it down.

Be grateful you disgust him, the victim in her hissed.

Grace realized with a shudder that she was so tired of being a victim. So tired of being afraid. So tired of being glanced over. So tired of the pain. So tired of feeling ugly.

So tired.

"Your thoughts are wrong," the angel whispered with a squeeze of his fingers, causing Grace's eyes to snap open. "You do not disgust me."

For a moment, the angel looked shocked that he had spoken such a thing. In fact, he looked as though he wished he could take it back, but then his eyes trailed down from her face. She felt them burn her as they grazed her neck, her collarbone, and then stopped on her breasts.

A look of pure masculine hunger flared in the angel's eyes, and his fingers tightened on her ankle.

A pool of heat spread in Grace's lower belly that was not unpleasant. She felt her nipples pebble under the angel's stare. Her breasts grew heavy and achy. She felt herself blush and quickly laid her right arm across her breasts, hiding them from view. The angel's glance skittered downward, and Grace covered the apex of her thighs with her left hand, shocked at the heat that radiated from that part of her body. She wished she had a third hand with which she could cover her belly.

He seemed enthralled with where her left hand lay, and after several moments, looked into her eyes again. "You do not disgust me," he repeated, his voice so deep it vibrated through her body. This time, it seemed like the understatement of the century.

She looked away and bit her bottom lip as lust hit her hard. She sucked in a breath at the onslaught, and heard the angel groan.

His fingers twitched against her ankle, and then she felt his hand slide upwards, trailing lightly over her calf.

Her eyes snapped to him. Instead of fear at his touch, for the first time in Grace's life, she felt sexual anticipation.

"I know—" He hesitated, and then tried again. "I think I can end your hurt," he said softly, every syllable tight and controlled.

His hand reached her knee. His fingers were so warm, and they were rough. The calloused skin tickled and scratched in a way that took Grace's breath away. His fingers moved to the inside of her thigh, and lightly trailed up, up. Grace felt a tremor pass through her body and noticed that she was having trouble catching her breath. Her erratic attempts to do so echoed in the air.

He laid his warm hand across the hand that covered her patch of curls, and Grace's body jumped. He gently took hold of her hand and began to move it aside.

Unbidden, memories of that night flew into her mind. Seth's body crushing hers. The terrible weight of him. The invasion. The feeling of being trapped. Grace's body tensed. Froze.

Immediately, the angel's hand lifted. "Shh." She felt him move from where he sat at the foot of the bed. The pain that his touch had abated flooded back in, and with it, panic.

"No!" she begged. "I'm sorry. Don't leave." She felt tears course down her cheeks. "Don't leave." She opened her eyes to find him beside the bed.

His eyes flooded with agony. "Oh, Temptation." He moved slowly, sitting by her hip and then laying down next to her. Looking at her carefully, he placed a splayed hand across her stomach. Instantly the pain fled. "I was not going to leave you," he whispered, his breath caressing her cheek.

The pressure of his hand changed. She followed the urging and turned to her side, facing away from him. She felt him slide in behind her back, not quite touching her, but the heat of his body poured over her. The hand on her stomach brushed a small, soft circle from her rib cage to the cradle of her hips.

"You are not trapped," he said quietly, right behind her ear. "Your body is your own. We are only giving it back to you."

Grace realized with a start that he assumed a position that did not have her pinned down. She was on her side. He was barely touching her. Every movement he made was soft and hesitant. His hold light. If she wanted to get away, she could easily slip from beneath his arm, jump over the side of the bed, and run out of the room.

His hand continued that light, circular caress, and Grace felt her fear vanish. He knew of her past, and his actions were the greatest gift he could have given her, speaking of both understanding and a desire to help her through.

Grace felt the tension drain from her body. And the second the last of her fear disappeared, the lust rushed back in. Suddenly, that light, innocent caress over her stomach was anything but light and innocent. It made her *burn*.

All of her longing for the angel on her shoulder, all of the passion she felt for him over the last few days, all of the times she gazed upon his body—it all rushed in at once.

With courage Grace did not know she possessed, her left hand fell from its protective spot over her sex. Her right arm uncoiled from around her breasts and moved downward, coming to rest over the angel's where it snaked over her side. She placed her hand on top of his, and her body took over. She began to drag the angel's hand down her stomach and toward the apex of her thighs, her heart thundering in her chest. "T-touch…me?"

She felt his body jolt behind hers. Heard him suck in a breath, the air stirring over her cheek. And then he groaned from deep within his chest, the sound causing the bed beneath them to rumble. He stirred, moving into her back until his chest rested against her shoulder blades. The contact of his smooth, cool robe and the heated muscle it encased against the skin of her back nearly did away with all of her inhibitions.

Him too, apparently, because his hand quickly moved the rest of the distance. The moment his fingertips encountered her curls, his body began to shake.

"Soft," he whispered into her hair. "So warm." His fingers moved again, and Grace's hips flexed on their own, canting forward and causing his middle finger to slip between the folds of her sex.

Her nails dug into the skin of his arm. "*Angel,*" she moaned.

His body went rigid at her back. The small tremble of before grew until he was shaking so hard, the bed began to creak. "Temptation…I want to hold you." His right arm tightened where it fell over her hip. "May I hold you?"

She felt her head nod frantically.

He sighed with what sounded like relief, and then his left arm gently worked its way under her body until both of his arms were around her. He pulled her back against him, her body lying flush against his. His left arm curled up and around until his hand brushed against her breast. He palmed the aching flesh and squeezed gently. She felt his breath brush against her neck, and then his face buried in the space between her neck and shoulder.

He embraced her, his arms tightening. His lips parting against her skin. "My Temptation," he breathed. He then held still for a few moments.

Grace realized he was giving her the opportunity to adjust to his new hold on her body. She still did not feel trapped. There was no fear, but there was distress of a different kind. Again, her hips jerked, and again, his finger slid against her slick flesh. "*Yes,*" she moaned as his finger caressed the bud at the top of her sex. She moved her hips again, needed the movement to be repeated. When she moved them the third time, his finger moved as well, sweeping down to meet her frantic thrust.

With a cry, she arched her body against him. Her ass came into contact with his firm, hard shaft, and for a moment she froze. She felt the angel hold his breath, and then she ground her ass against him, wrenching a sudden, shocked noise from the angel.

"*Human*," he groaned. And then he seemed to snap.

His arms, though still gentle, tightened. He pulled her hips firmly into his erection, and his fingers slid deeper into the space between her thighs. She moaned as he circled the area over and over that he had already discovered was her most sensitive, but she wished for more. She flexed her hips forward, desperately hoping he would take the hint and trail that talented finger lower. He only held her tighter; moved the finger faster. Before madness could take her over, she covered his hand with hers once again, and moved it slightly to the place where she ached for him the most.

His powerful body, already strung so tightly behind her, stiffened even more. She could feel his heartbeat pounding between her shoulder blades. And then, after only a slight hesitation, he slid his middle finger inside of her body.

A sound close to a sob tore up through Grace's chest, and the angel made a noise halfway between despair and paradise. He cupped her fully, his thick finger filling her, and she tried to cry out from the pleasure before she burst, but it was so intense she couldn't gain her breath. He ground the heel of his hand against the spot he could no longer stroke and began to thrust his finger in and out of her body as he began to rock his hips into her, his shaft grinding into the small of her back.

He began to mumble a stream of incoherent words into the moist flesh between her neck and shoulder, and Grace caught random words here and there: *beautiful, Temptation, control, need.*

The desire in his voice drove Grace to the edge. A tight spring was wound within her belly and getting tighter with each one of the movements his hand made. His hand squeezed her breast again, and then she felt his teeth scrape her shoulder. "Angel!" she cried as the tension within her snapped. Her body bowed and shook as her passion overtook her. She felt her sheath clamp down on his finger over and over again. His groan was one of utter pain as he froze and pulled her in tightly.

The waves of her orgasm began to abate, and Grace could breathe again. The angel still had not moved. His hand remained frozen between her legs. In fact, the only indication that he was alive was his harried breathing, and the small, distressed moan he gave at the end of every exhalation.

For the first time in days, Grace's body was at peace. No—it was better. She had no idea her body could feel those things. *Do* those things. She turned her head to look at him. He withdrew his face from the crook of her neck and met her eyes.

Grace gasped. His honey-green eyes were…*glowing*. That was the only way she could think to describe them. And abject misery covered his face.

Those eyes traveled down from hers to her lips. He stared hard, and then he licked his bottom lip and began to lower his head.

Grace sighed and licked her own lips as she began to close her eyes. Anticipation boiled through her. She could swear his lips would be the most wonderful she ever touched—

He jerked.

Grace's eyes popped open when, with a violent growl, the angel whipped his hand away from her sex and leapt from the bed.

He stood a few feet from her, his chest billowing, and stared in disbelief at his glistening fingers. His eyes flew to hers once again, and she read such need, such emotion. And then, without another word, the angel turned from her and sprinted toward the door, flinging it open and disappearing into the hall.

Chapter Eleven

The Compulsion hammered within Jayden's brain. It was hungry—so hungry—for completion.

But, a different hunger, a different longing for completion, overshadowed even that. A hunger so powerful, Jayden almost lost himself.

Every fiber of his being yelled at him to turn around. To return to her. To rejoin her in the bed. To plunge within that sheath that had clamped around his finger, milking him.

He stumbled down the hallway, his hand, covered with her desire, held aloft. His arousal bobbed painfully. He lurched into his room, throwing himself inside and slamming the door behind him.

He fell to his knees. With a roar, he grabbed his robe with his left fist and tore it up and over his head, flinging it aside. He looked down at his naked body. His knees were spread wide apart. Every muscle in his thighs was bunched and angry. His arousal sprang from between them, jutting heavenward. The muscles in his abdomen quivered.

He looked again at his right hand. It was still covered with *her*. Her essence glistened in the dim light. With a cry, his hand flew to his arousal, wrapping around it. It was still warm and slick from her sex, and he tightened his grip with a groan.

Following an instinct he had only recently discovered he possessed, his hand began to move, pumping up and down, his grip tightening, his fingers passing over the sensitive nerve endings.

Every time his fist passed over the aching head, he cried out. His seed began to rise, filling his shaft even more.

He closed his eyes and threw his head back. He pictured his woman. His Temptation. The way her skin glowed. Her perfect, rose-colored nipples as they pebbled for him. The way her body flooded with moisture when he touched her entrance. The way she sighed and moved against him.

Her eyes.

With a guttural yell, Jayden climaxed. Stars flew behind his closed eyes as he felt his seed shoot over his hand and splash his chest and abdomen. "*Grace!*" Her name flew from his lips as pleasure unlike any he had ever known wracked his body.

The pleasure faded, and Jayden was able to take a deep, healing breath for the first time since entering her room a lifetime ago.

Clarity.

He looked down at his body. Evidence of his folly covered his torso. With a sigh, he grabbed the sheet from the nearby bed, dragging it toward him and cleaning the spent passion from his chest.

And as he slipped his robe over his head once more, Jayden realized the most disturbing part of this incident: Though he felt a measure of regret, he wasn't sorry. And he would do it again.

With a grimace, Jayden slowly stood, a heavy weight about his shoulders keeping him from moving quickly. Every bone in his body hovered between the utter relaxation his first orgasm had given him, and the kind of tension that foreshadowed unwelcome change.

He bent over to pick up the blanket he had used as a towel. He crumpled it into a tight ball and clutched it to his belly with a convulsive swallow. What was he to do with it? He could not leave it here where any of the humans could find it and learn of his unforgiveable weakness.

Something within his chest lurched in protest. To call this act an unforgiveable weakness was accurate, and yet did not feel right. It cheapened it somehow, this handful of moments that Jayden would never forget.

He plodded to the door, his wings drooping behind him, and opened it to stick his head out into the hallway. A quick look right and left, and then Jayden forced himself to move with some measure of speed toward the supply closet. He exhaled in a whoosh when he made it to the closet without any encounters, and was even more relieved when he discovered a laundry bin beneath a shelf of extra linens. He could put the blanket there, shove it down to the very bottom where no one would ever—

"Jayden."

Jayden spun around with a very un-warrior-like intake of air, twisting his arms to hide the blanket behind his back.

He felt the blood drain from his face and fought for calm. "Anahita," he managed hoarsely.

She stood close enough for him to see the shocked flare of her eyes at his uncharacteristically distant greeting. She was as beautiful as all of his brethren: robed in white, flowing hair, perfect features, breathtaking wings, and a purity that Jayden himself no longer possessed.

Shame poured hotly down Jayden's throat, and he fumbled for the laundry bin without sight, dropping the blanket and slamming the door of the closet before leaning against it and praying that she would not ask—

"What are you doing?"

His first thought was of utter thankfulness that Anahita's gift from the Most High was teleportation, not telepathy. Long moments passed as Jayden mentally scrambled for something to say that would be plausible. He arrived at nothing, and then realized that her presence here did not bode well. "What are *you* doing here?" he asked more defensively than he wished.

Her face remained emotionless. *Because she knows her duty*, Jayden mentally chastised himself. It had been mere days ago that Jayden possessed that same distance, that same blessed lack of emotion.

Her voice was soft and free of the censure Jayden deserved. "I was sent to check on the status of your mission, brother. To see if you required help."

"No!"

This *did* garner a reaction. Anahita took a small step back, her lips parting slightly.

"No," Jayden said, softer this time. "I require no assistance." And then, because he needed to be reminded as much as she needed to know, "The most grievous defiler is with child. I must wait for her to deliver. Then I can carry out my mission."

Anahita's face relaxed. "Of course, Jayden." She offered a small smile. "The others will be relieved. They have been worried."

Jayden's stomach dropped to his sandaled feet. The others would only be worried if—"They have talked to the Most High?" Jayden had taken so long that the Most High had decided to intervene? That had not happened in centuries.

"No, brother. Things have not yet gotten so dire."

Before relief could fully take its hold, Jayden felt a flare of very human jealousy. Jayden had not heard the Most High's voice in ages. The Most High rarely spoke to His angels, but He spoke to the defilers all of the time. Jayden heard Him speak in their thoughts, and it nearly killed Jayden. Words of encouragement. Words of love—

Jayden straightened. *Words of love?* If the Most High loved the humans, then why was Jayden here? Why was he ordered to kill them?

Jayden searched his memory. Since that first time so long ago, the Most High had never again confirmed Jayden's mission. Only the other angels, his commanding officers, continued to communicate the necessity of slaying the defilers of the Tree of Eternal Life.

A sick foreboding filtered into Jayden's consciousness. The Compulsion forced an angel to complete a mission, whether or not that mission was commissioned by the Most High. Lucifer had decided on his mission alone and followed his own Compulsion into the pit of hell.

Jayden was doing the right thing. *Right?*

"My brother?"

The quiet, uncertain question pulled Jayden from his thoughts. He dragged heavy eyes from the floor to look upon one of the few beings he called friend.

"My brother, are you well?"

Jayden shuddered. Was he well? He did not know. Had he somehow allowed himself to fall from grace? Had he gone rogue without realizing it?

"Jayden," Anahita said, her voice rising slightly, "your mission is right. Holy. You know this." She reached out to squeeze his bicep, the friendly touch only making Jayden wish the hand belonged to someone else. "Do not allow the presence of your Temptation to cause you doubt."

Jayden jerked his arm from her grasp, wrenching a shocked gasp from his fellow angel. *She knew.* She knew that Jayden faced his Temptation. It was obvious enough for them all to see, humans *and* angels.

Love makes one weak.

"I know," Jayden ground out between clenched teeth. "I know my mission is holy. I *will* carry it out." *The Compulsion will make sure of it, whether my mission truly comes from Most High or not.* Jayden shoved the bitter, distressing thought aside. He could no longer dwell on that possibility. The brief time he had spent pondering it already chipped away at Jayden's peace of mind.

Anahita stared silently at Jayden for several moments before speaking again. "If you should need me—"

"I will not."

Anahita's mouth snapped closed. Her eyes swam with doubt. "Of course, brother."

In the next second, she was gone.

Jayden closed his eyes and rubbed the ache in his chest with an open palm. Who knew what report she would carry back to their commanding officers?

Who knew what Jayden would do now?

Chapter Twelve

Over the past three days, Grace had trained with the angel all day, every day. She was shocked at how good the physical activity made her feel about herself. She was even more shocked that, for the first time since she was seventeen, she felt safe. And while under hostage. She'd been sleeping better lately. Well, better if the heated dreams her constant physical contact with the angel created didn't count.

In fact, since that first time he had shown her some simple self-defense moves, she hadn't once had a nightmare about the attack. And if her thoughts touched upon the attack during the day, she was easily able to steer them in another direction.

For the first time in thirteen years, Grace was free.

But, as Abilene and Dahlia had warned, she developed a severe connection with the angel in their time together. Dahlia put her on birth control, much to Grace's horror. "Trust me," the woman said patting her growing baby bump. "Practical matters don't register in the heat of the moment." What was worse was that Dahlia seemed to be right.

To her libido, it didn't matter that the angel was keeping her prisoner. All it cared about was that the angel was near. Laying his hands on her, even though her mind often reminded her libido it was only for the purpose of teaching Grace how to fight. No other reason.

But then the angel's eyes would flare as his palm skimmed down her arm, and Grace would wonder.

Their interaction in the past few days also convinced Grace that the angel was telepathic. No sooner would one of their encounters bring an unwelcome flicker of her memory to the attack than the angel would back off. Completely drop his hands from wherever they touched her and apologize, making sure to give her plenty of physical space.

At first, it embarrassed Grace to a devastating level, but in the ensuing days, she had grown thankful, and now she had done a complete turnaround so that when he pulled his hands from her body when her thoughts turned, she was actually disappointed. His touch provided the perfect distraction. Not to mention how wonderful his hands felt on her. Having them withdrawn was a punishment.

Her longing for him had gotten so bad that, in her daily meeting of her sexual need, she had grown completely unsatisfied with her own touch. She wanted *him* to touch her. To bring her pleasure again as he had that one time—a time that featured prominently in her fantasies ever since.

But at this rate, with his quick apologies and immediate removal of touch, she would never know what it felt like to have him bring her pleasure again. And that was beginning to be a problem.

Today, the angel was teaching her how to throw an enemy. She hadn't even laughed this morning when he'd announced that was the plan. She'd grown to trust him in ways she would never have guessed. One thing was certain, if the angel said something, it was true. If he thought she could actually throw an enemy much larger than herself, she believed him.

Even still, she had been shocked when she'd first managed the feat shortly after breakfast. She would never forget what the angel looked like landing flat on his back with a dramatic *umph*—the fact that he exaggerated the effects of her moves had not escaped her notice. But, perhaps, her moves *would* have that effect on a mortal man who would no doubt be much weaker than he was.

"Now," the angel said, drawing Grace from her thoughts, "let us do it again, this time with the attacker holding a weapon."

Without thought, Grace's attention flew to the hilt of the sword where it appeared over the angel's right shoulder. It was always strapped to his back, never out of his sight. She got the impression that he both expected the humans to be afraid of it and to try to steal it at any moment. But Grace wasn't afraid of it. She had studied it closely for a handful of months. To her, the sword was like an old friend.

Nevertheless, as soon as the angel noticed where her eyes wandered, *he* blanched. "No," he said quickly. "Not an actual weapon. We shall…*pretend*."

So, the angel didn't want to wield the sword against her, even when it was not as a real threat? *Interesting*.

He moved the lesson on quickly, as though he needed to distract her from noticing his reaction. "Most humans are right-handed, so we will begin that way, though we will practice both." He already stood before her, so he didn't move except to raise his right arm, his hand clutching an invisible weapon. "We shall assume this is a blunt object. We will do knives later, but imagine this is a stick of some kind. Notice all of the space I have created here." With his free left hand, he gestured to the open part of his body at his right side. "This is where you go. Stop my arm with your left forearm."

She stepped forward and followed his direction. It placed her directly in the shelter of his body. She was staring at his Adam's apple as it bobbed briefly.

"Good," he said, his voice cracking. "Now hook your right arm up and around and grab my shoulder from behind."

She obeyed. It felt wonderfully like an embrace. Her face was all but buried in the muscle between his bicep and shoulder, and it took all of her willpower to keep from rubbing herself against him like a cat.

He didn't speak for a few moments, and she wondered if she was doing it wrong, but then he said, "Now, I am off balance because my weight has been thrown into a strike. Use that to your advantage, Temptation."

Annoyance edged in on what Grace was feeling. He never once addressed her by her name, usually calling her human. But he occasionally referred to her as *Temptation*—and she'd learned it was one of the ways he tried to keep her at a distance.

"Notice how your hip is directly behind mine. Butt against me and at the same time pull my shoulder back."

She did it quickly, her movements rougher than she'd intended as she acted out of stung hurt at being called *Temptation* once again. It worked better than she'd thought the move would work. He went flying, his legs all but shooting out from under him. She seemed to have legitimately caught him off guard—she *had* moved before he'd even finished the instruction—because she went down with him. That had never happened before. He was always so in control of where his body went that she had more than enough time to extricate herself from his body as it fell.

This time, she fell forward, emitting a very unladylike squeak as she rushed toward the floor. Moments before she face-planted on the tile, his hands shot out and grabbed her, pulling her safely to his chest. She face-planted in the middle of his pecs instead.

The world completely froze as she assessed her current position. She was sprawled directly on top of his body, pressed against him fully. Her hands were planted on the floor on each side of his ribcage. His arms held her loosely; his hands were resting, one in the small of her back, the other between her shoulder blades. They were warm and so large they left very little of her back untouched.

It was exquisite.

She turned her face to the side and rested her cheek against his chest. His heart was thundering. And then the hand between her shoulder blades moved slowly and gently up until it grasped her nape. His other hand moved as well, allowing him to wrap his arm around her. His arms tightened.

He was hugging her.

She felt every muscle in her body relax, causing her to sink into his body further. She was afraid to breathe, lest he end the embrace, but she did dare to rub her cheek against his chest.

It felt so good. *So different from Seth*, she thought.

As soon as the thought entered her brain, the angel moved. His arms suddenly vanished. He grasped her loosely around the upper arms and tried to set her on her feet.

Frustration charged through her. "What are you—?"

He shifted beneath her until she was no longer lying on top of him but sitting on the tile, and then he abruptly shot to his feet and took two giant steps away from her. "Angel, *stop*!"

He did, tilting his head to the side and staring at her with obvious confusion.

"I didn't…want you to…move," she said haltingly, feeling a blush spread to the roots of her hair.

He frowned. "But you thought of him. The one who hurt you."

Grace barely refrained from a blurted '*I knew it!*' So the angel did read minds. Great. Just her luck. She looked at the floor, mortified beyond belief that he was able to discern her thoughts.

She heard him move forward, and then his finger was beneath her chin. He gently turned her face upward. He was crouching before her. Emotions she couldn't identify flickered in his eyes. "Will you tell me of him, Temptation?"

She jerked her head back. His hand fell. "Will you tell me why you call me *Temptation*?" she spat.

His eyes hardened. A muscle ticked in his jaw.

Grace smiled without warmth. "Exactly how I feel, angel. Besides, don't you already know everything about him? About all of it?" She'd thought of it enough in front of the angel. She would be surprised if any aspect of her rape remained a mystery to him.

His expression told her she was right. "I find I wish to hear it from your lips," he said.

"Why?"

He sighed. "I do not know."

Well, at least she wasn't the only one confused by the desires she felt around him.

"A trade?" The words came from *her* to her surprise. Since they were already out there, she continued with, "I tell you what you want to know," she had to swallow past the lump in her throat, "and you tell me what I want to know?"

The angel grimaced, but several seconds later he nodded tersely. She was shocked. Never in a million years would she have thought he would agree to such a thing. He must desperately want her to tell him of the attack if he was willing to give up just one of his secrets in exchange.

"You first," she said.

He smiled. "I think not."

Her mouth snapped open. "But you could decide not to tell me anything after you hear!"

He gestured to himself. "Cherubim, Temptation. We cannot lie."

It was his use of that obnoxious word again that finally made it happen. "Fine!" But after a few wasted moments, Grace realized she didn't know how to start. It had been thirteen years since she'd told anybody. With a feeling of helplessness, she raised her eyes to his.

The amber green depths warmed, and he sat beside her, crossing his legs. "How old were you?" he prompted.

Relief that she wouldn't have to come up with the tale completely on her own flooded her. "Seventeen."

Though he had to have already known, he made a small, angry noise. "So young." His voice dripped with sorrow.

"He was my first—and *only*—boyfriend." She paused. "Actually, I guess I can't call him that. It was all a joke anyway. There was a bet going around school that no one could get the fat girl to give it up," she tried to laugh, but it came out choked.

She felt his big hand land on her back, and he began to stroke a sure, slow circle between her shoulder blades. It gave her enough courage to keep going. "When things didn't move as fast as he wanted, when he'd decided that I really *wasn't* going to sleep with him, he decided to take it." She began to shake. "His friend helped. Held me down so—" She broke off. That was as far as she could go. The most she could tell.

After several seconds of silence, the angel said, "Shh," even though she hadn't spoken in a while. "You do not have to tell me more."

No, because he already knows it all, she thought sadly. *Knows how it felt. Knows what I was thinking when he forced himself into my body. Knows the fear I've had of men ever since.*

His hand moved from her back to her shoulder, and he tugged her toward him gently, giving her a squeeze as she fell into his side. "You will never have to go through that again," he said seriously. "I will make sure of it."

It was too much. Grace pushed away from him and turned on him with confusion and not a little bit of anger. "I'm sorry. Are you serious? Aren't you planning on *killing* me eventually?"

Anger flickered in his eyes, too, before fizzling out to be replaced with something that looked like shame. "I am no longer planning on it, no."

Something in his tone did not set Grace at ease. "It sounds like it will still happen," she said.

He turned sorrowful eyes upon her. "It will."

She narrowed her eyes. "I think it's time you tell me something now."

He sighed, and turning his face to the wall so he wouldn't have to look at her, spoke. "All angels have one thing they will encounter that they will find nearly impossible to resist. Something put on earth to test their loyalty. Their strength. For some of us it is power. Others, wealth. For me—" he turned to her once again, "it is you. Creating life with you is how I Fall. You are my Temptation, human." He smiled sadly. "And I call you such to remind myself of what I stand to lose if I am weak."

The fact that Dahlia had put Grace on birth control flashed through Grace's mind unwelcome, rendering her mouth dry. "And what do you stand to lose?"

He laughed without humor. "Everything." He lifted a hand and trailed a finger gently down her cheek. "My heart."

Grace felt like she couldn't breathe. A million new questions burst through her mind. "But you say you *will* kill me?"

His hand dropped back to his side, his eyes shuttering. "I did not tell you I would reveal *all* of my secrets." He smiled again, albeit sadly, to soften his words. "My promise is fulfilled."

And so it was. But even so, Grace could not prevent one more comment, "I do not like it. Being called *Temptation*."

He looked at her with concentration for a moment, and Grace realized he was probably reading her thoughts again. She allowed how she felt when he called her such a callous thing to flood her mind.

He broke eye contact. "I did not know it hurt you. What would you have me call you instead?"

She huffed. "My name! You know what it is."

"I do."

"So you will use it?"

He looked at her again, and if she didn't know better, she would swear he was feeling panic. "I—" He closed his eyes for a moment, and then opened them, an odd determination shining from within. "I do not wish you to call me *angel* any longer, either."

"Okay," she said, unsure at his abrupt change.

"I am called Jayden."

Grace swallowed hard. He'd just told her his *name*. She hadn't realized until this moment how much she'd longed to know it. It was beautiful. Strong. Tantalizing. Just like the angel himself. She took a deep breath, knowing how big a deal this must be for him. Then, looking deep into his eyes, she repeated it back to him. "Jayden."

His pupils dilated immediately, and he moved so quickly she hadn't known he had until his hand was again on her cheek, cupping her jaw. "I liked that," he said, his voice deep and rough.

Obviously, she thought.

He apparently picked up on the thought because he gave her one of those unpracticed smiles. His thumb brushed across her bottom lip, and his brows drew together as his eyes focused on her lips. It was more than apparent that he wished to kiss her. Though he'd pleasured her with his fingers, he'd never kissed her. "It's okay," she whispered.

He jumped, his eyes flicking up to hers in question.

"You can kiss me," she said on a barely audible breath.

His eyes widened and then jetted back to her lips. His attention was doing things to her body. She felt her breasts grow heavy, the apex of her thighs grow damp. If he didn't kiss her, and soon, she didn't know what she would do. "Jayden," she whispered, the word a plea.

He moved, leaning in so slowly it made her heart ache. His breath caressed her lips first, and then he brushed his mouth against hers so lightly she wouldn't have known they'd kissed but for the violent clenching of her stomach.

He pulled back slightly and groaned from deep within his belly. He licked his lips and closed his eyes. Then he scooped her up in his arms. The next thing Grace knew, they were seated. His back was against the wall, and she was in his lap, her shoulder pressed against his chest, his arms firmly around her.

He leaned her back across his left arm, and his right hand came up to her face again, brushing her cheek as his fingers burrowed into her hair. "So delicious," he whispered.

His lips descended again. This time, his kiss was firmer. He pressed his lips against hers fully for several seconds before lightly brushing them back and forth.

It was an innocent, inexperienced kiss, possibly the sweetest Grace had ever experienced, and yet it shot straight from her lips to her womb. She moaned softly and wrapped her arm around his neck, pulling herself closer to him and pressing her breasts against his chest.

His arms tightened, and he kissed her again. Urgency marked this kiss. His breathing quickened. Grace felt as though she would explode. She opened her lips slightly and skimmed her tongue across his bottom lip.

His entire body jerked violently. His head snapped back, and Grace worried for a moment that she had done something wrong, but then she looked into his eyes. They were molten. He stared at her lips with wonder. "*Grace*," he breathed.

The use of her name pounded into her. With a hungry noise, she pulled his lips back to hers. He met her more than halfway. This time, his lips were open, as were hers. They breathed for each other for a moment, and then he tentatively repeated the kiss she had just shown him, sweeping his tongue across her lip.

Grace moaned and sucked his tongue into her mouth. With a groan, he followed her lead as she taught him to duel with their tongues. He quickly learned what she liked, and within moments, she needed him so badly, she thought she would die.

Just then, he pulled away. His breaths panted across her moist lips. His eyes held a question.

Gathering all of her courage, she said, "Jayden, could we—would you," she blushed fiercely, "touch me again?"

Chapter Thirteen

Jayden stared at her, dumbfounded. Her thoughts had been insistent, but he had not dared to believe he was interpreting them correctly. And now she was asking him to—

"Touch you?" he asked breathlessly.

Her blush deepened. "Never mind," she said quickly.

She had! She had asked him to touch her! "Yes," he blurted quickly, hoping it was not too late. The possibilities roiled through him, and he nearly groaned. "Oh, Grace, yes."

Her embarrassment morphed, softening her eyes and lips as she smiled shyly at him. "Really?"

"Yes," he said again like an idiot.

Her smile took on a twinge of humor. "Maybe in a room?"

With shock, Jayden realized they were in the hallway. Where either of the other two humans could happen upon them at any time. He shot to his feet, cradling his woman in his arms and fighting down an unidentifiable emotion. A sound like the snapping of a bed sheet echoed through the space, and his wings unfurled like a shot and curved around her, placing them in a cocoon of beautiful, iridescent feathers. No one was allowed to see Grace like this except for him. The thought was fierce and right.

She turned wide eyes upon him. "No one can see me?" she asked, her tone tinged with awe.

Jayden shook his head.

She sighed, snuggled into his arms, and rested her head on his shoulder. He quickly nuzzled her cheek with his and then carried her into the room where he had been spending the night hours as the humans slept. He could have easily gone into her room, but some primal part of him wanted her in the small space he claimed for himself.

She pulled her head back and gifted him with a smile. He returned it and trailed a finger from her cheek to the neckline of her shirt. "Will you take this off for me, Grace? I wish to see you," he said deeply.

Doubt filled her eyes, and Jayden cursed inwardly. *Too fast*, he scolded himself. He shushed her, and then he placed his lips softly over hers, cradling her close and taking whatever she would willingly give.

Her fingers flexed on his shoulders, and she pulled back to whisper, "Can I see you, too?"

He sucked in a breath. "You wish that?"

She nodded her head. He sensed she was still nervous about revealing herself to him, but her desire to see him bare had her considering it. To cover his desperate hope that she would gift him with the sight of her body, he turned her face toward his and kissed her again. He meant to be gentle, but the kiss quickly morphed into the passionate embrace they had been sharing in the hallway. The next time he had enough self-control to remember to check her thoughts all of her nervousness had vanished.

He deepened the kiss even more, instinct telling him to probe her mouth with his tongue deeper than the shallow sweeps she had taught him minutes ago. She responded with a moan and returned the kiss wholeheartedly. His fingers returned to the neckline of her shirt, and she pulled back slightly, hesitatingly raising her arms. With more fumbling than he would have wished, he was able to raise her shirt up and over her head while keeping her cradled against his body within one arm.

As soon as the shirt left her body, she made a small noise of discomfort, and Jayden tightened his wings around them, blocking out a majority of the light. She relaxed a fraction, and

Jayden let her shirt drop to the floor unheeded as his entire world narrowed down to Grace's gorgeous chest. She wore a simple white undergarment over her breasts. Jayden's mouth went utterly dry, and he raised shaking fingertips to brush across warm, firm swells.

Grace gasped. As Jayden sensed a majority of her anxiousness disappear, she arched in his arms, thrusting her breast into his palm. He rewarded her with a gentle squeeze, and then she was wiggling in his arms fiercely.

"Let me down," she whispered against his lips.

He let her feet touch the floor, but only unfurled his wings slightly, not willing to quite let her go. And there, within the shelter of his wings, she finished the job he had begun with her shirt. Reaching behind her back, she unclasped her undergarment and clutched the slackened garment to her breasts. His heart, which had moments ago stopped within his chest, began thundering. He had seen her bare before, but this was the first time she unclothed herself for him. Specifically *for him*.

Just when she was going to let her undergarment slide from her shoulders and to the floor, she looked at him expectantly, her eyes flicking down to his robe as she arched a brow.

He flicked his wings away into his back. She made a noise of sorrow when their shelter vanished, so he quickly tugged his robe over his head, let it drift to the floor, and then surrounded her once again with his wings.

He smiled down at her, but discovered he was staring at the crown of her hair. Her head was tilted down, and she was staring silently at his groin.

His eyes followed hers down, and he saw his body, primed and ready for her. His arousal was bigger than it had ever been when he was by himself. Her eyes upon it seemed to make it swell even more. It kicked up, jerking under her stare, drawing a gasp from her.

Jayden quickly felt for her thoughts and was disappointed to find the nervousness had returned.

"I don't think I'm ready for—"

He saw where her thoughts were headed and felt relief. She was not ready to have sex with him. That was convenient. He was not prepared for what having sex with her would do to his entire existence either. Despite her beauty, despite her hold on him, Jayden could not Fall for her.

But her nervousness ate at his heart. He did not want that emotion anywhere in her mind when she was with him.

With a finger beneath her chin, he lifted her eyes. He waited patiently for her to look at him, and when she finally did, he instinctively knew drawing attention to his own inexperience in this matter would put her at ease. "I am not ready for that step either, Grace."

Her eyes widened. In her thoughts, she remembered that Jayden would be a virgin.

"I will only touch you. Like you asked," he said. "I promise."

She looked at him in disbelief.

"Cherubim, remember?" he reminded her. "You say the word, and I walk away. On my honor."

She relaxed, and then smiled at him hesitantly. Her thoughts told him she was worried she had ruined the mood.

Hardly. Jayden had a feeling nothing would ever keep him from wanting her. He felt a twinge of worry as the Compulsion rolled over within his gut—reminding himself that he had to keep whatever emotional distance he could from her. What little emotional distance remained.

She stepped toward him, pulling him from his thoughts, and wrapped her arms tentatively around his middle, pressing against him.

He swiftly enfolded her in his arms, seeking to assure her he was still here with her. Still more than ready to bring her to pleasure, but then all thought fled.

Her shirt was off. The small garment across her breasts was the only barrier between his naked chest and her warm skin. He pulled her in tighter and heard himself make a small noise. "You feel wonderful," he breathed.

She tilted her head back and smiled up at him, her relief obvious. "So do you."

He moved his hands slowly, giving her time to protest, to her shoulders where he gently pushed the straps of her undergarment down her arms. She stepped back slightly, looking at the floor. She blinked as the slip of fabric fell away, but did not cover herself.

Jayden's moan was deep and guttural. She was so beautiful Jayden's chest ached.

She remained quiet as he gently lowered her pants and the undergarment beneath them. She stepped out of them.

And then she was completely naked, standing within the shelter of his wings.

She closed her eyes briefly, and Jayden felt the doubt she had been holding at bay breach her mind. She began to move her hands to cover her breasts, but Jayden cupped her face with both hands, gaining her attention and stalling her movements.

"You are beautiful, Grace." His voice was so deep, so hoarse, he almost did not recognize it.

He monitored her thoughts carefully, and she recalled that he could not lie, and then her doubt diminished, though it did not entirely vanish. He would just have to work hard to make sure that it did.

With that in mind, he kissed her, quickly swooping in and giving her no time to think further. As he deepened the kiss, she sighed into his mouth and stepped close once again, wrapping her arms around his neck. Her naked body pressed against his fully for the first time.

His arousal was cradled between their bellies—hers soft, his hard. Her breasts were pressed into his rib cage right beneath his pectorals. He could feel the heat from her sex against his thigh.

With a hiss, he broke the kiss. "*Grace…*" The sensations the touch of her body brought were unlike anything Jayden could have imagined.

She brushed her fingers through his hair, smiled, and pulled him down for another kiss. As he thrust his tongue into her mouth, he walked them backward until the bed hit the back of her thighs. He gently lowered her until she lay on the bed, and quickly followed her down, stretching out on top of her, resting his hips between her thighs.

His arousal pressed against the sleek heat of her sex, and they both froze. Jayden remained frozen only for a second, and then he wrenched himself away, turning to the side. He lay on his back beside her in the narrow bed and cast his forearm over his eyes as he tried to control his breathing, which echoed through the room like an oncoming army.

He had scared himself. For a moment there, he had been primed to plunge into her body. His arousal had been at her entrance. Even now, he could feel the slickness of her body on his shaft.

Every instinct in his body had urged him to make her his in every way. And he had almost done so. *After* promising Grace he would not.

"Are you okay?" Her voice sounded small and concerned, but completely devoid of fear. A quick survey of her thoughts showed him he had not scared her, and that should have brought relief.

Instead, he could not feel anything other than the raging want coursing through his body. "Need you so badly," he muttered before he could stop himself.

He felt the light pressure of her hand on his chest. Felt her lean in. Her breath caressed his cheek. And then, in his ear, she whispered, "*Good.*"

His eyes popped open in surprise, though he could not see anything through the arm still resting across his face. Her hand started to move down. Her fingers trailed over his stomach, and without hesitation, wrapped around his arousal.

His arm fell from his eyes. His back arched as he groaned to the ceiling. "*Highest heaven.*" It felt so good, he could not see straight. The contrast between her soft palm and his calloused one was night and day. And then she moved her hand, slowly stroking up from base to head of his shaft.

Blindly, he turned his face toward hers; kissing anything he came into contact with—her forehead, her eyelids, her cheek—as he sought her lips. She continued to stroke him, and he finally found her mouth and plunged inside, groaning against her lips with every movement of her hand.

That peak he had reached so many times on his own as he thought of her loomed over him, and he realized she was going to bring him to orgasm, quickly, if he did not stop her.

"*Grace*," he gasped, pulling slightly from the kiss, "slow down." She had to be there with him. He turned onto his side, facing her, his hand moving to her hip and stroking down.

"Am I doing it wrong?" she asked anxiously.

He groaned. "*No*, I am. Your soft hand is going to make me finish before I take care of you."

His fingers reached her sex, and he brushed through her folds seeking and finding that nub that brought her to pleasure before. She gasped, and softened against him.

"Wrap your arms around my neck," he whispered urgently, touching her deeper, spreading the slickness of her arousal with his fingers.

She did as asked, and with his free arm, tunneled beneath her body and hauled her in close. His shaft pressed against her belly, and his hand fully cupped her sex. He kissed her as he slid a finger deep inside her body, grinding the heel of his hand against her most sensitive spot. And then, his body took over, canting his hips forward, thrusting his arousal against her soft, warm body.

Shivers of pleasure wracked him, and he repeated all movements over and over.

Soon, he could tell she was reaching her peak. She began to moan into their kiss. Her arms tightened around his neck, and she rubbed her breasts against his chest. Jayden's world tilted violently as he struggled to outlast her, the need to spill his seed threatening his control. He thrust his finger deeper, ground the heel of his hand faster. And, thankfully, it worked.

Her body began to tremble. She jerked back from their kiss to stare into his eyes. Hers widened and then closed as she cried out his name and arched against him.

It pressed his shaft more fully into her belly, and finished him as well. "Grace," he groaned as his seed shot from his body. He pulled her even closer and buried his face in her neck, pressing an open-mouthed kiss to her pulse as she undulated into his hand. Her sheath clenched and re-clenched his finger in flutters. Moisture spilled into his palm.

It was the most amazing thing he had ever experienced. Even before he was capable of complex thought once again, he knew it to be true. He was made to bring this woman pleasure.

Her body relaxed. She breathed a soft laugh as she loosened her grip upon him, softly skimming her fingertips over the welts her nails had left behind—marks that he would have gladly borne, but that would sadly be gone in seconds.

And then her breathing changed. Grew regular. She had fallen asleep.

Jayden lay still and listened to her breathing and her heartbeat for an eternity. She felt so good, warm and soft in his arms. His eyes began to close in sleep. He wanted to hold her while she slept. To stay here with her. Forever.

His eyes jerked open in shock. *Forever?*

It was that word that made him move. He gently but quickly extricated himself from her and left the bed. She moaned softly and stirred, her eyes blinking open sleepily and staring at him with confusion.

"Jayden?" she asked in a sleepy voice.

His heart stuttered in his chest, but he turned from her and walked toward the door.

"You're not staying?" Her voice was filled with hurt, as were her thoughts as they flooded him.

He stopped at the door to sweep up his robe, but refused to turn around and look at her. "I cannot, Grace," he whispered. *Because I want to more than anything in the world.*

"But—"

Whatever she was going to say, he did not stay to find out. He silently left the room and closed the door behind him. With a shuttering sigh, he leaned back against the door, held his robe against his naked, still-hard shaft, and fought heaven and hell against the desire to join her again. To crawl into bed with her and calm the doubt now running rampant through her mind. But if he ever had a hope of not dooming himself, he could not. *He had almost fallen asleep.*

As for his heart—he had thought joining with her completely would damage him irreversibly. He had underestimated the connection he would create with the actions they had just taken. His heart ached more than a physical wound, and Jayden worried that he had already lost it.

Chapter Fourteen

It was an unbearably long night for Grace. After Jayden *left* her, with no more explanation than *I cannot*, Grace hadn't been able to go back to sleep. She hadn't been able to do anything but examine her actions for a misstep.

Which only infuriated her. *He* acted crazy, and she was ready to blame it on herself? That was not something Grace had been willing to do for well over a decade.

Lying in his bed—though why he had a bed when she was pretty sure he didn't sleep—was disconcerting to say the least. More than a dozen times throughout the night, she wished she could just get up and leave. But if she was in his room, he had nowhere to go but the hallway, and she just couldn't face him right now.

The words *walk of shame* came to mind.

But now it was past nine in the morning. She never stayed in bed past six, and she had been training with Jayden each morning shortly after that. She could hear Jericho and Dahlia up and about and knew her time of self-imposed quarantine was coming to an end.

With a sigh, she sat up. She was already dressed. That had happened seconds after Jayden had closed the door behind him. She couldn't stand being naked in the bed one second longer. She'd scrubbed the evidence of his orgasm from her skin with one of the blankets that now lay crumpled in the corner. *Let him deal with that.*

She walked with leaden steps to the door, and when she opened it, it took all of her presence of mind not to gasp.

Right across the hall, leaning up against the wall and watching the door without blinking was the angel. His arms were crossed, as were his ankles. His wings were out and hunched around his shoulders as though for warmth. When she opened the door, he straightened, dropped his arms to his side, and stared at her without saying anything.

Awkward....

That was when he spoke. "It was not your fault."

That was what he chose to respond to? Of all the things she had been thinking, he chose to narrow in on the brief second she'd allowed herself to ponder if his leaving were her fault? "I know that," she spit acidly.

He frowned in that way men do when a woman has acted in a way they can't interpret. The tilt of his head told her he was trying to read her thoughts again.

She forced her mind to blank and stared at him as hostilely as she could.

He frowned and tilted his head even more. After a few seconds, he straightened, shock clearly flashing across his face. Then those luscious lips split into a wide grin that caught her off guard. "Good for you, Temptation."

She resisted the urge to stamp her foot. Temptation? They were back to that, were they?

"I knew you were a natural warrior," he said. "I am proud of you for analyzing the situation—correctly—and defending yourself."

She frowned. She was disturbed by how much his praise meant to her.

But he wasn't done. "Time for training," he said seriously. "Now."

There was an urgency to his words that she had not heard in his tone before, and it unsettled her enough to agree without argument, though the idea of resuming their routine had horrified her a mere minute ago. She followed him silently to the large part of the hallway where they had been sparring. Something was about to change, she could sense it.

Still, she was shocked when he turned to her and removed his sword from where it rested on his back. It flickered blue briefly before returning to the beautiful green and gold flames it usually sported. He held it loosely with both hands in front of him.

She eyed him warily. "What—"

"Today's lesson," he said softly. "I will strike with the sword. You will disarm me."

• • •

She gasped. "Are you serious? Disarm you?"

Jayden was more than aware that he was crossing a line. In the back of his mind, he knew he was teaching her how to defend herself. Against *him*. When the Compulsion grew too strong, and he turned on her.

Fortunately, he was still so proud of her for ascertaining that he was trying to read her thoughts and blocking him that it overpowered the guilt his current actions created. "Yes."

He raised his sword over his head. The action, even though for the purposes of sparring and teaching her how to disarm him, made him sick to his stomach. Her eyes grew wide as she looked at the sword poised to strike. Oddly enough, he discovered she was not scared. Of the sword or of him. In fact, she had a great deal of respect for the sword. She thought it...*beautiful*. His stomach lurched again. "Arms up," he commanded more roughly than he intended.

She seemed to snap out of a stupor, her eyes snapping back to reality. She raised her arms above her head.

"Cross your wrists," he said with a suddenly dry mouth. Her breasts rose so tantalizingly beneath her shirt with her hands to the sky like that.

She crossed her wrists and waited for his next instruction.

"When I swing down," which was usually the way he struck in battle, "catch my wrists with the vee of yours." He swung wide before she could question, and she followed his directions beautifully. He showed her how to direct his momentum downward and then elbow him in the chest to get him to drop the sword.

As soon as she had done it successfully, he barked, "Again." He made her repeat the move until she was breathless and perspiring, but could pull the move off without a thought.

"Good," he whispered.

Her breasts huffed up and down. Tendrils of her red hair fell from her ponytail. She was so beautiful. And though she could disarm him now, she did not do so without his compliance. Jayden knew she did not stand a chance against him when he was actually forced to take her life. When the Compulsion took away his free will.

He heard a noise and looked up to find the other two humans standing in the hallway looking at Grace and him with questioning eyes. Their thoughts were a cacophony of shock, and the undeniable knowledge of what Jayden had truly been attempting to do. The blond—*Jericho*, he mentally corrected—looked at him with softness in his eyes for the first time in days.

Jayden shrugged at Jericho helplessly as he re-sheathed his sword. The sorrow that his attempts to avoid the inevitable had done no good was too great to allow Jayden to speak.

A loud boom sounded directly behind him. They all froze. It took a fraction of a heartbeat for Jayden to realize that someone—a *lot* of someones if the thoughts were any indication—were attempting to breach the rubble of the cave-in.

Helplessness settled in on Jayden's shoulders like a burial shroud. He realized with a pang that he did not wish to stop them. They were a group of soldiers whose goal was to rescue the three humans from their captor. It was something that Jayden had just been attempting himself.

Jericho approached him and laid a hand on Jayden's forearm. Jayden tensed, expecting an attack from this side of the rubble as well, but when none came after several seconds, Jayden read the man's thoughts.

He was using the Knowledge on Jayden. Was hearing the word *good*. Jericho looked into Jayden's eyes and smiled. "It will be okay, angel," he said gently, squeezing Jayden's arm before removing his hand. "What would you have us do?"

Jayden stared at the man in amazement. He was in earnest. Another boom sounded from the rubble, and several of the smaller rocks fell from the pile and pinged off of the floor. A few seconds more and they would breach the medical wing.

"Capture me," Jayden blurted out. Jericho's eyes widened. "Quickly," Jayden said, falling to his knees and crossing his wrists behind his back. "Put me some place secure." As the Compulsion bellowed inside Jayden's head, he allowed himself to look at Grace once more, and could not keep his eyes from raking her body one last time, knowing all he felt for her was written plainly on his face for all of them to see. Knowing he was revealing his weakness. "Just promise me you will keep her away from me," he said to Jericho while not taking his eyes from his Temptation. Her eyes widened. Her hurt flooded over him. "And make sure I can never get out."

It might work. Lord of the Most High, it might work. If they were able to secure him, he could save her. The impending separation from her knifed through him with a pain so sharp he winced and looked away from her.

"You mean it?" Jericho asked, doubt dripping from his voice.

Another boom. They were nearly here.

"Now!" he ordered.

Dahlia rushed down the hall and returned with a length of rope from the utility closet. Jericho quickly bent and tied Jayden's wrists together. He felt as his sword changed color, the flames growing hot where they flicked against his back as it anticipated trouble.

"Grace," he barked at her without allowing himself to look at her, "take cover."

She hesitated. "Jayden—"

He turned to Jericho. "Drag her away from the rubble if you have to."

That got her to move. She brushed past him to stand by Dahlia in the shelter of an open door, trailing her fingers along his shoulders as she did so, causing Jayden to shake. The last time she would touch him. Why she would even do so given his behavior, he had no idea, but he was grateful.

The rubble exploded outward, and Jayden turned his face into his shoulder as pebbles of all sizes hit him, cutting flesh that immediately began to mend.

The soldiers charged in, but stopped in their tracks as they caught sight of him. He was positioned on his knees right at the medical wing entrance, his hands bound behind him, Jericho standing at his shoulder.

Jericho laid a hand on his shoulder, and gave an indiscernible squeeze meant to comfort. "The angel has surrendered," he said in the voice of a soldier not to be questioned. "He is ready to be taken into custody."

Eli stepped forward, an apology in his eyes. A quick scan of his thoughts told Jayden he had tried to stop this rescue attempt. Had thought Jayden would not hurt his friends. The man's faith in Jayden humbled him. He looked down as Eli and Jericho communicated with the wordless language of true friendship, and then Eli said, "Okay, men, take him to a cell."

"The most secure we have," Jericho said with a meaningful look at Eli.

The other man nodded, and then two soldiers moved forward. One reached for his wrists, ready to wrench him to his feet. The other reached for the hilt of Jayden's sword, meaning to disarm him.

Jayden immediately began to struggle. He did not know why he had not anticipated this move. Prisoners were always disarmed. But they could not take his sword. Not with Grace standing feet away. He was already at the edge of his control with holding off the Compulsion. Taking his sword would trigger it. He could feel it down to his bones.

He broke the rope binding his wrists with one swift tug, and launched to his feet. The soldiers who had been standing behind Eli immediately rushed him, piling on top of him one by one. Jayden remained on his feet, a dozen men hanging off of him. He turned in panic to Jericho. "They cannot take my sword." He tried to convey all the disaster that would ensue if they tried with his eyes. "They cannot."

Jericho quickly barked, "Let him keep the sword. Who can he hurt in a cell?"

Eli quickly corroborated the order, and the large pile of soldiers on Jayden's back slowly slid off, each one looking sheepish. As soon as they stepped away from him, Jayden once again crossed his wrists behind his back, turning them toward Jericho and allowing the man to bind him once more.

Then, without a word, Jericho himself began to march Jayden out of the medical wing.

"Jayden!" he heard Grace yell from behind him. There was a brief scuffle, and Jayden knew Dahlia was keeping her from rushing to him.

He turned his eyes to Jericho. "You must keep her from me," he whispered urgently. "Forever. Send her away if you can."

Jericho smiled sadly and gave a reassuring nod. And then he walked Jayden through the open atrium where the trees stood and into a prison ward. They arrived at a cell so secure it would keep any human prisoner without the possibility of escape. With a swift perusal, Jayden knew it would not hold him if he did not wish it to. His shoulders drooped.

He had one hope left. That somehow, when the Compulsion struck, Jayden could maintain enough hold on his free will to keep from harming her. From harming them all.

Chapter Fifteen

One Week Later

Grace was losing her mind. She'd been apart from her angel for only a week, and she was losing her ever-loving mind.

She spent all of her free time in the observation room overlooking Jayden's cell. Jericho pressured her to leave the facility, but Grace had nowhere to go. She'd cultivated a nomadic lifestyle for herself—going wherever the work was. She had no new job. She had nowhere new to go.

After catching her in the observation room two days in a row, Eli even agreed to let her write up a much-edited findings for the language on the sword.

It was the career-making opportunity of a lifetime. And still, she was here, looking down through mirrored glass at an angel. She hadn't thought of her career in over a week. She couldn't ignore the possibility that she wasn't leaving the facility because this was where Jayden was, and she couldn't stand to be apart from him.

Losing. Her. Mind.

But, if Grace was losing her mind, it was nothing compared to what Jayden was going through.

That first day of his imprisonment, when Grace sneaked into the observation room while everyone was sleeping, she had found Jayden huddled in the corner, his body slumped on the floor. From her position above the room, she has gazed at his head where it was resting on his bent knees. He didn't move all night. And she couldn't miss the way his wings constantly trembled.

The next day, however, things changed. Jayden paced his cell with an impatience that was so thick, Grace could nearly see it. His hand kept jerking toward the hilt of his sword where it peeped up over his shoulder. And then he would growl and pace faster.

The next day, his eyes lost their focus. His pacing turned frantic and no longer followed a straight line across his cell.

He was in distress. That much was more than obvious. Not for the first time, Grace began to ponder the possibility that he had no choice in carrying out his mission to kill them all. It would explain so much: his reticence to have a relationship with her, his attempt to train her to disarm him, his plea that she be kept away from him.

The hurt that last part had caused had long since vanished as Grace had watched him struggle with himself.

Something much more disturbing was taking its place. The warm, desperate longing she had been feeling for Jayden while his hostage had been morphing over the past week. Several times in the past few days as she had been glued to the reflective glass, she caught herself feeling something very close to...*love*...for the angel.

She was falling for him. Alarmingly quickly. Time and separation were only making the feelings stronger.

Now, a full week later, she was again observing him as close as she could get to him in the middle of the night while everyone else was asleep. Her heart was in her throat as she watched him pace. His movements were primitive. Those of an animal. Whatever precipice he perched on, he was close to going over. He was frightening, and yet, Grace was not afraid of him. She was done being afraid.

As she watched, he changed the direction of his path again. He walked toward the door, his wings completely unfurled, and rested his forehead against the metal of the cell's top-security door. His entire body started to shake. His sword started to glow even brighter, the flames turning an ominous black.

But then he whispered. Spoke for the first time since his imprisonment. The sound was picked up by the hidden microphones in the cell and broadcast into the observation room. In a tremulous voice, Jayden whispered, "*Grace*. Where are you?"

His voice, broken and hurting, shot through Grace's body. She was running out of the observation room before she realized she left it.

The halls were blessedly absent of personnel, and Grace raced to Jayden's cell, the route burned into her memory from all of the times she'd traveled it in her mind. When she reached the hallway where his cell was located, she absently grabbed the master key from the guard's room, and then peeked around the corner.

The roving guard was just walking away from her, on his way past Jayden's cell. He would make a circuit of the square-shaped wing and be back at Jayden's cell in less than a minute.

Grace kicked off her shoes, and jogged silently on stocking feet to Jayden's cell. She arrived at the door just as the guard turned the corner. The key slid into the lock with an audible *snick*, and Grace held her breath, expecting the guard to have heard it and return any second to investigate.

Instead, Jayden's voice sounded from within. "Who is there?"

"It's me," Grace whispered as she turned the key.

"Grace? You are still here?" His voice was panicked. The lock clicked. "For God's sake," Jayden said urgently, "do not let me out!"

She had precious seconds left. Even now, she could hear the guard's shoes clacking in the hallway. Any moment, he would turn the corner and spy her breaking into the angel's cell. Without another second to waste, Grace pushed the cell door in, rushed past the doorframe, and shut the door behind her as quietly as possible.

After a few seconds of tense silence, Grace turned slowly to find Jayden right behind her. His eyes were focused for the first time in days, and they were staring at her with unidentifiable intent.

For a moment, Grace was nervous. But then Jayden's expression cleared, and he reached for her, jerking her into his body and crushing her against his chest. "Oh, *Grace*," he whispered fervently into her hair. "I thought I would never see you again."

His heart thundered in his chest, and with his touch, Grace felt her world shift into focus. She wrapped her arms around him and hugged him close, breathing easily for the first time since watching him hauled away with his arms bound behind him.

• • •

He could not stop pressing kisses into her hair. He knew he was squeezing her too tightly, but she was *here*. In his arms once more, when he had thought to never have such an experience again. She was returning his embrace. Rubbing her face against his chest. He felt like he was going to burst apart.

Even the gut-wrenching fear he felt when he discovered she was still in the facility was no comparison to the joy he felt at having her returned to him. She gave him sanity. For the first time since his imprisonment, he was thinking clearly. The Compulsion, which had been racking up and down his spine and clawing the inside of his head for days, was now humming in the distance. She was centering him. Bringing him back to himself. He felt as far away from *weak* as he had ever been.

All of the times he had wished to lay with her and denied himself now reared up in his memory, and he cursed them for the missed opportunities they were. Why? *Why* had he kept himself from her in that way?

She cleared her throat and spoke into his chest. "Dahlia put— I'm on—" She sighed, and Jayden stroked a hand down her back to sooth her. "I am safe," she finally said. "I'm taking something that will keep us from creating life together." She buried her face further into his chest, and Jayden froze.

That was why he kept himself from her. His Fall. He should feel relief. He could be with her and not get her with child. Would that keep him from Falling? Obeying the letter of the law but not the spirit?

Jayden did not know. In fact, he only felt a painful pang at the thought that she would not carry his young—the proof of his love for her.

He loved her.

His body's lack of any surprised reaction told Jayden he must have loved her for quite some time. Peace—the last emotion he would have expected in the face of such a revelation—settled down into Jayden's soul.

Unable to keep himself from tasting her any longer, Jayden placed a finger beneath her chin. He raised her head.

She looked at him with those beautiful gray eyes, and he saw the same desire he felt echoed in her gaze. It was a flame licking up his spine.

His shaft grew hard instantly, filling and pressing into her belly. She could not miss it, and her eyes fluttered closed, and she sighed happily through parted lips, rubbing against him with her hips. Jayden lowered his head.

She seemed to sense him, for even though her eyes were closed, she tilted her head as his lips descended. At the first sweep of his lips against hers, they both sighed. Their open mouths fit together, and Jayden swept his tongue inside, needing to taste her as deeply as possible. *Needing to taste her.*

The thought struck and planted in fertile ground. He lifted her gently within his arms, and walked slowly to the bunk that he had not once used since being closed in this room. As he walked, she wrapped her arms around his neck and sucked his tongue even deeper into her mouth, twining hers against it with a sharp sound of desire.

He lowered her so she was sitting on the edge of the bed, quickly kneeling between her knees, allowing her to keep her arms around his neck. Her lips on his. Without sight, he sought out her buttons and removed her blouse and undergarment. Knowing she was bare from the waist up was exquisite torture, but he could not even consider breaking their kiss to look, the need to taste her the most severe of feelings.

But then, she pulled from the kiss and began trailing her lips across his cheek to nibble on his jaw and then brush kisses down the column of his throat.

He tilted his chin up with a groan, allowing her better access. He wrapped his arms around her, splaying his hands on her back and drawing her close. Every sweep of her hot tongue, every brush of her soft lips driving him to insanity. He ran his hands over her exposed skin, touching her with gentle slowness. Though his desire to possess her was so intense, he shook from it; he would not touch her with any measure of roughness.

He knew intimately the violence with which she had been introduced to sex. He would never allow that to be even a shadow of her experience with him. And so, he moved slowly. Knowing he could savor her, and in so doing, make the experience good for her.

He dipped his head and found her lips again, gently pushing her back into the mattress and leaning forward with her, crowding into the space between her spread knees and lying flush upon her breasts. Her softness met his hardness at every angle. And then, he began to kiss her cheek, moving to her neck just as she had shown him moments ago.

Her fingers tangled in his hair as she clutched him close. His fingers found the zipper of her pants and worked it down. Without breaking the kiss, he swept them and her underwear down her legs. With her pants gone, her knees spread even wider; his body surged into the valley of her thighs. His shaft pulsed against her sex, the moisture and heat of that part of her body penetrating his robe. Before he could forget his intent at the sensations shooting through him, he moved his body, slowly sliding down to kiss her collarbone. Her breasts.

He paused to languidly suck each nipple into his mouth briefly before descending further to press kisses down her ribcage. To swirl his tongue around her belly button, which made her belly quiver and her knees shake, much to his delight.

When his kisses dipped below her belly button, her fingers tightened in his hair, and she tugged fretfully. Jayden quickly scanned her thoughts and saw no fear, only embarrassment. He would not allow her to be embarrassed of this. He slowly but insistently pursued his downward path, arriving at last at his intended location. He nuzzled her auburn curls, and when she tried to close her knees self-consciously, he redirected her legs over his shoulders.

"Jayden?" she asked nervously.

But he barely heard her. She was spread open right before his face—the first woman he had ever seen like this. The *last* woman he would ever see like this.

And she was *exquisite*. So pink. So swollen. So wet. He swept his index finger down the center of her folds, and her body leapt. She jerked to an upright position, but he held her legs firmly, keeping her just where he needed her. He looked into her eyes.

"I love you," he said, no longer able or willing to keep his feelings to himself.

She gasped in disbelief, but before she could say anything, he bent his head while keeping their eyes locked and placed an open-mouth kiss right over the bud that lay at the top of her sex, throbbing for him.

She made a small noise in the back of her throat and closed her eyes.

He pulled away to say, "*Watch me*, Grace."

Her eyelids fluttered open again, and she turned her unfocused gray eyes upon him. Confident she would not look away, he dipped his head again, further this time, to gently penetrate her, briefly sticking the tip of his tongue into her opening, then pulling it up and over her bud. She moaned long and low, her body trembling. She shifted her weight to the side and braced herself with one hand. With the other, she stroked her fingers into his hair, cupping the side of his face, looking at him with... *love*. She was looking at him with love.

"Oh, *Grace*." Her name was a groan. A plea. He fell forward, burying his face in her sex. He slipped his hands beneath her bottom and pulled her close, loving the pleasure of this intimacy. Of being so close to her.

Her fingers sifted through his hair. He kissed her bud once again.

Her sigh was one of want. He would deliver. He began to lap her, flattening his tongue and passing it over this center of her pleasure. He created a steady rhythm he knew she would love, a rhythm she had shown him before. He looked at her again, and with his eyes, he implored her to not break their visual connection. It was a beautiful gift. He did not miss a moment, as her eyes grew rounder and rounder. As her body shook harder and harder. As his tongue took her over the edge. As she cried out. As her eyes flooded with tears and she stroked his face while undulating beneath his mouth. As her body softened. As her hand caressed the back of his neck. His shoulder.

He turned to kiss the inside of her thigh, and straightened. He wanted to love her with his body now. Returning her soft smile, he slowly pulled his robe over his head.

Her smile turned completely lecherous as she reclined upon the mattress again, and crooked a finger at him.

He brushed his hands up from her knees to cup her breasts, kneading softly. She arched her back into his touch, and the movement pressed her sex against him.

His shaft fell directly on her cleft, the head sliding up through the moisture his mouth had created to brush against the bud. She moaned and pressed against him again. It was unlike anything he had ever experienced. Her body was hot and slick and perfect. He leaned forward and gathered her up in his arms. Rising slowly to his feet, he brought her with him, directing her with his hands to wrap her legs around his waist. She was embracing him with her whole body, and he wanted—needed—to be closer.

His wings circled them, holding her as close as his arms did. His feathers brushing across her skin and raising goose bumps. They were looking into each other's eyes when he clutched her bottom and repositioned her. He was so hard, he did not have to position himself; he just naturally perched at her entrance. With his other hand, he cupped her cheek and stroked his thumb across her bottom lip. "Never doubt I love you, Grace," he whispered. "You are my first. My only." He leaned forward and pressed his forehead against hers, their eyes a breath apart. "*My everything*."

Then he slowly flexed his hips and lowered her body onto his shaft. Inch by inch, he filled her, entering a woman for the first time in his existence.

Her sheath clenched tightly around him. The heat. The softness. Every inch of her stroked him in ways he could not believe. He glided in to the hilt, his body shuddering, the sac between his thighs tightening. The pleasure was so great he had to close his eyes. Focus intently to control the urge to thrust once more and empty himself inside of her. *So tight!*

But she whispered, "Watch me, Jayden." The echo of his earlier plea made him smile.

He opened his eyes and stared into hers. "Lord of the Most High, you are so beautiful," Jayden breathed.

She closed the distance between their lips, sweeping her tongue across the seam. Inviting him to penetrate her here as well.

His arms began to shake as he slipped his tongue between her lips. At the same time, he tightened his arms, lifting her. She flexed her thighs where they hugged his waist and helped him withdraw his shaft and slowly enter her again.

With a shuddering sigh, she buried her face in his neck, nipping him gently. "So *good*," she whispered, her breath tickling the damp skin and wrenching a groan from Jayden's chest.

His arms tightened even more, holding her as close as possible. One hand slipped up to cup the back of her head and cradle her face against his throat. The other hand tightened on her bottom once more. Then he began a slow, steady rhythm of thrusts.

She began to make the most tantalizing noise in time to his movements. A mix between a gasp and a moan each time he filled her body fully. And then, when he was seated to the hilt, her sheath would squeeze him. Milk his shaft. It was pleasure so intense, his eyes rolled back into his head.

Control of his breathing entirely abandoned him. He realized he was panting as he began to move her body slightly quicker. Her breasts rose and fell, brushing against his chest deliciously as he worked her up and down on his arousal.

Her noises abruptly cut off with a startled, "Oh."

Her sheath began to flutter along his shaft. She was about to peak. In answer to this knowledge, his own body surged toward completion, his seed pooling at the base of his shaft.

He wanted to watch her face. He pulled back, encouraging her with the hand to her nape to lock eyes with him. Her eyes were wide and unfocused when they met his. He brushed his nose across hers and thrust into her one final time.

She cried out, her eyes widening even more. And then, breathing his name, hugging him close, she sank down on his arousal even further. Her body seized around him. Her inner muscles clamped down.

Jayden groaned. Every muscle in his abdomen contracted. His seed surged. He crashed his lips onto hers to muffle his cry, thrusting his tongue inside her mouth as his seed shot into her womb. Stars danced behind his eyes.

His heart swelled.

With a shaky breath, Jayden ended their kiss with one final press of his lips to hers. She smiled at him softly and nuzzled against his neck once again. He pressed her close in one last embrace and then carried her over to the bed. He lowered her to its surface and followed her down, refusing to leave her body.

"Make me invisible again?" her sleepy voice asked.

He pulled back to look into her eyes. "You could never be invisible, Grace."

Her eyes drifted closed on a sigh. Jayden kissed her forehead and rolled to his side, a heaviness settling into his eyelids. He wrapped his arms and wings around her, and together they slept, Jayden slumbering for the first time in his life.

Chapter Sixteen

Grace woke to the sounds of a soft snore. It took her a few moments to realize where she was, but the warm, firm muscle beneath her cheek was a dead giveaway.

She was in Jayden's cell. In Jayden's arms. And he was snoring.

Grace felt her cheeks stretch in a grin. She snuggled into Jayden's chest even more, throwing a leg over his hips.

Her body jolted as the inside of her thigh encountered a part of the angel's body that was definitely *not* sleeping. "Oh, *God*," Grace breathed as she moved her leg, stroking him with the sensitive skin of her inner thigh.

Immediately, she wanted him again. She felt herself flood with moisture and muffled a groan by burying her face in his chest. Images of their lovemaking just hours ago flashed behind her closed eyelids. He'd held her aloft in his arms, his wings wrapped around her, and rocked his body into hers until he'd brought her to the most gentle, sweet orgasm she could have ever imagined.

But right now she felt anything but gentle and sweet. Details she'd noticed but not dwelt on now came to the forefront of her memory. The way his muscles had bulged in his arms, shoulders, and chest as he had moved her body up and down his cock effortlessly.

She shivered. *Delicious.* She opened her mouth and licked the valley between his pecs. A field of goose bumps erupted on his skin. Grace's head snapped up to look at Jayden's face. The angel slept on, though his body reacted to her closeness.

Grace smiled, the beginning of an idea forming. She smoothly slid her body onto his, straddling his hips without jostling him awake. She silently congratulated herself.

And then she was completely distracted by the view.

God, but her angel was magnificent. Here perched on his hips, his erection wedged snugly against her clit, she could look down on him and see his gorgeous body uninhibited.

His face was turned toward the side, his lips inches from where her head had been moments ago, giving the impression he had fallen asleep with his kisses pressed to her hair. Her heart lurched, and her eyes traveled down the column of his neck, to the hollow of his throat, to his torso.

Slabs of muscle covered him from shoulder to hip, creating the most beautiful landscape of man Grace could have ever imagined. His dusky brown skin was warm as syrup, and from memory, tasted as sweet. His flat nipples were erect; his chest still dotted with the goose bumps her lips created. As he breathed in and out slowly, his abdomen dipped and rose, creating sharp ridges of muscle. Good lord, the man had an *eight* pack.

She couldn't keep from touching any longer. A careful eye on his closed lids, Grace leaned forward, running her palms up from his stomach to his pecs. She splayed her fingers across the muscles of his chest. The muscles leapt beneath her fingers, but other than a flutter of eyelashes, those honey-green eyes didn't open.

His big hands, however, *did* move. They trailed up from the sheet to rest on top of her thighs. He squeezed her legs in his sleep.

Grace felt an answering ripple in her belly, and more moisture pooled between her legs, spilling out onto his erection. His fingers tightened on her skin, and his breath caught. His eyes remained closed.

Oh, this was deliciously wicked, this seduction of a sleeping angel. Very slowly, she rocked her hips, moving back and forth once on his shaft. Spears of pleasure shot up from the friction he created against her clit, and she couldn't prevent a sound from escaping her lips.

His eyes popped open, full of sleepy un-focus. Slowly his head turned, and those green eyes came to rest upon her. Naked. Straddling him. "Grace?" he asked in a sleep-rough voice.

"You were sleeping," she said, and then she rocked over him again.

A harsh grunt erupted from his chest. His fingers clenched on her thighs. "Sleeping?" Disbelief dripped from his tone. "Is this a dream?"

He looked so endearingly confused. Grace couldn't help the bubble of joy that surged up through her. "No, angel, this is not a dream." She rocked on him again, and all of the sleep vanished from his eyes. They focused on her sharply, quickly raking down her naked body. She felt everywhere his eyes touched like it was a caress.

God, when he looked at her, she felt *pretty*. Something she never thought would happen.

"*Heaven*, you are beautiful." Sleep now gone, his voice filled with awe. His hands rose from her thighs to cup her breasts. His thumbs swept across her nipples, wrenching a small cry from Grace. She arched into his touch, feeling an urgency to join with him.

He gently squeezed her breasts, but Grace needed more than gentle. She slid forward until the head of his erection was at her entrance. Leaning down and bracing her hands on his chest, she canted her hips and shoved back, taking him inside of her to the hilt with one quick movement.

She slammed her eyes shut and cried out. Loudly. A sound she heard him echo. She felt her core seize on his shaft, and hissed through her clenched teeth as she fought with all of her strength to keep from coming right away.

His hands abandoned her breasts and grabbed her ass. His hold was almost rough, and it was obvious he was preventing her from moving again. She opened her eyes.

His face was inches from hers. His eyes were wide and horrified.

That wasn't right. "Jayden?" she asked softly, feeling unsure.

"It…f-felt so good," he stuttered, sounding panicked. "And then you cried out. You clenched your teeth. God, Grace, I *hurt* you. I am so sorry."

Hurt her? Grace felt her heart crack right in two and then fuse back together, stronger than ever. Her angel, so wise, so implacable, was nonetheless innocent in what happened between a man and woman. She smiled down at him and stroked his face. "Oh, Jayden, you didn't hurt me."

His eyes narrowed skeptically. She leaned down and pressed a kiss to his grim lips. "It *did* feel good. That's why I cried out. You cried out, too, you know."

"I—I did?"

"Oh, yeah," she straightened and found his grip on her ass had loosened enough for her to move again. "It was *sexy*," she purred.

His lips tipped at the corners slightly, and Grace shoved back again, thrusting him inside of her roughly. He gasped. Bit his lip. Every muscle in his body froze, and it was more than obvious that he was afraid to move.

"It doesn't always have to be soft between us, angel," Grace said gently, twisting her hips side to side.

"I…never want…to hurt you," he said haltingly through clenched teeth. "Your past—"

Her cracked heart fused together again and felt as though it swelled right out of her chest. He was gentle with her on purpose. Because he wanted to show her he was different from Seth. "Is my past," she finished for him, rising on her knees and slamming back down.

"*Grace!*" he shouted, tipping his head back. Every muscle in his torso flared into sharp relief. "Oh, no," he breathed.

His hips bucked beneath her, and she felt him shoot hotly inside of her. "Oh, God," she moaned. She'd made him come. "*Oh, God,*" she said again as his entire body shuddered with the force of his release. She rocked her hips in time to the jerking of his, drawing his orgasm out as long as she could.

It was the most pleasurable moment of her life. And she hadn't even come herself.

His body finally stilled beneath her. She stroked his chest, licked her lips. She was still so desperate for him. He slowly tipped his chin back down and looked at her with eyes flooded with shame.

"I am sorry," he mumbled, his eyes canting to the side. "I tried to stop it. You felt...too good." His eyes returned to hers, his brows drawn together. "I left you behind, love."

She shrugged one shoulder. He had. But it had been *so* worth it. "I *loved* it," she whispered, leaning down to press her breasts against his damp chest. She couldn't resist kissing him. Thrusting her tongue within his mouth.

He was quick to wrap his arms around her back. To return her thrusting tongue with his own. She moaned into his mouth, her need rising even higher. Her core clenched, and she gasped in surprise, wrenching from their kiss to stare into his eyes. "You're hard!" she breathed.

How was that possible? Thank *God* it was possible!

"Always for you, Grace," he whispered, pressing a soft kiss to the tip of her nose.

And then her world blurred as Jayden flipped them. Grace was suddenly on her back, the angel still hard and filling her, his hips between her upraised thighs. "So," he said with a sexy smile. "You like it harder, hmm?" He withdrew from her until only the tip of him remained. Grace sucked in a breath. "I find I like it as well."

He slammed forward, his hips slapping against her. He ground himself against her sex, wringing bolts of pleasure from her clit.

"*Jayden!*"

He stilled and stroked her face. She opened her eyes again to find him looking deeply at her. "You swear this is okay—"

In answer, Grace tilted her hips away and slammed onto *him*. He groaned, tossing his head back. His arms seemed to collapse, and he landed on her, crushing her breasts, slamming his lips onto hers, thrusting his tongue into her mouth.

Between her knees, she felt him withdraw again and then thrust hard. Withdraw. Thrust. He picked up a fast, brutal rhythm that Grace's body was helpless to resist. She wrapped her legs around his waist and met him thrust for thrust. Her fingers dug into his shoulders and then moved south to where his wings sprouted from his back. She brushed her palms over them, and Jayden cried out, tearing his lips from hers and burying his face in her neck. He bit down on her collarbone and thrust even faster into her.

Wings…sensitive, her passion-addled mind determined. She stroked them again, and his entire body jolted. He made a loud sound of distress and worked his hand between their bodies. "Cannot do this…*again*," he groaned into her damp skin.

His thumb found her clit, and as he thrust harder, he circled her firmly.

Grace flew apart. She screamed his name. Digging her heels into his ass, she bucked against him. Waves of pleasure hit her again and again.

He bellowed into her neck, slammed into her one last time, and she felt his ejaculation pour into her. "Oh, Grace," he groaned. "Oh, *love*." His thrusts slowed and finally stopped.

He didn't raise his head, and their breaths were so loud and fast they echoed through the room. Grace's knees fell, and she wrapped her arms around him fully, stroking his back and wings. "I love you," she whispered.

He lifted his head slowly and met her eyes. The honey-green she adored darted back and forth as he looked from one of her eyes to the other.

"I love you," she repeated.

His entire face lit up. A wide grin spread. "I am so glad," he said hoarsely. He buried his face in her neck once again, heaving a shuddering sigh. "I am so *happy*," he breathed.

Grace smiled, hugged him close, and slipped back into sleep.

Chapter Seventeen

Grace jerked awake. Her eyes flew open. She was immediately aware of three things: she was cold, naked, and alone in the bed; Jayden was dressed and standing before her; and his sword was pressed to her throat.

She could feel the heat of the metal. The licking flames. The blade so sharp she was afraid to breathe lest it cut her.

Her eyes jerked from the weapon to the angel wielding it. He was still breathtakingly beautiful. He stood before her, robe cascading down the body she had thoroughly loved. His wings flared behind his back. His hair flowed around his face and shoulders. His face was a blank mask. "Jayden," she breathed, moving as little as possible.

"Do not say my name, defiler," the angel growled.

Terror rushed through Grace's body. She looked closely at Jayden's eyes. The warm, honey green was gone. In their place was black. All black, from corner to corner, lid to lid.

Jayden her lover was no longer here. In his place was an avenging angel.

With utter clarity, Grace realized she was about to die. That the precipice she had sensed the angel had been poised upon over the last week had finally been breached.

On instinct, Grace scrambled back away from the sword's blade, dragging the sheet over her nakedness. The blade followed her movement, and she froze when her back hit the wall.

Nowhere to go.

The flat of the blade touched her chin, forcing her to raise her face to his and stare into those heartless black eyes.

"You have eaten from the Tree of Eternal Life," the angel said in a stranger's voice. "The punishment for such an offense is death. Prepare your soul."

Intense sadness leaked into her heart. Sadness for herself, yes—for the first time in thirteen years, she wanted to live. But also, sadness for Jayden, who would snap from his stupor upon her death and see that he had killed her.

Her agony would be short-lived. His would last forever.

Compassion she did not know she could ever possess for an attacker filled her soul. *Her* Jayden would never do this. He was having something taken from him by force as well. She felt her terror lessen. Her eyes softened. She looked at the angel she loved with all of her heart. "Angel," she whispered to him, "it will be okay."

Those cold, black eyes narrowed. The blade beneath her chin wavered. A tendril of green honey swirled over black. "Grace?" the angel asked in Jayden's voice. Green flooded the black, and suddenly, Grace was looking into her Jayden's eyes once again.

They widened with horror. The sword shook even more. "Grace," he whispered desperately. "*Run!*"

• • •

Jayden watched as her face blanched. He held onto this moment, this rare moment of control, with every fiber of his being. He had to give her the chance to get away. If he could just hold the Compulsion off for a few precious moments.

The human launched herself from the bed, dragging the sheet with her. She flew to the door of the cell and pounded on the metal. The booms echoed through the room. "Help me," she screamed. "Somebody, help!"

The Compulsion pressed. Jayden pressed back.

And lost.

The world shifted into shadows and light. His gaze narrowed. Focused on his prey. The defiler continued to bang on the door as he stalked forward. He raised his sword, zeroing in on the space between her neck and shoulder where he would strike.

The place where he loved to kiss.

His steps stumbled. He shook his head, dislodging the errant thought.

The defiler spun from her pounding and looked upon him with wide, gray eyes. One lone tear escaped and trailed down her cheek.

He raised his sword higher, braced his feet, and prepared to swing.

Like a gasp of air, Jayden broke through the Compulsion. "*Kill me!*" he commanded her before losing himself again.

His arms bunched.

He struck.

Air whistled past his blade as it closed in on the defiler's neck. The job was almost done.

Her arms shot up. They caught him at his wrists mid-swing.

With a final shove, Jayden pushed aside the Compulsion at this vital moment, and tempered his strength enough to allow her to redirect his blade. He dropped it even before she elbowed him to the chest just like he had shown her to do.

It clattered on the floor.

She lunged for it, picking it up by the hilt and turning toward him. She pointed the sword at his chest.

The Compulsion beat against his brain, urged him to give in and allow it to complete the job.

"Do it," Jayden hissed through gritted teeth.

The sword wavered. Her eyes flooded with more tears. "I love you," she whispered.

Not more than I love you. The pain in his skull became unbearable. He had no time left. Without another word, Jayden lunged forward, grabbing her hands and directing the blade. It slid into Jayden's chest and pierced his heart without a sound.

Grace screamed and jerked away.

The Compulsion finally faded, its absence causing Jayden to slump with relief. *Or is that pain?* Jayden looked down at his chest. Blood spilled from around the sword's blade. His fingers spread through the warmth that gave him life. He brought his hand away and stared at the crimson dripping from his fingers.

He was dying.

He looked from his hand to the face of the woman he loved. The one he would gladly have Fallen for, if only he still had the chance. Tears streamed down her lovely face. Wounded animal noises fell from her lips. He tried to smile for her, but doubted he succeeded. He closed his eyes.

I will never harm Grace. The thought brought him comfort.

I will no longer be able to protect her. Unimaginable sorrow.

His legs crumpled beneath him at the same time that the cell door burst open.

Shouts pinged off of the concrete walls as soldiers flooded the room, Eli and Jericho at the forefront. Dahlia ran to Grace and wrapped her in a hug, questions flying from her mouth at the speed of light.

Jericho and Eli knelt beside Jayden. Eli pulled the sword from Jayden's chest, and pain shot through his body. Jayden moaned, much to his horror.

But what was worse was how they all kneeled around him, shouting orders and questions and blocking his view of Grace.

He wanted—*needed*—to watch her while he died.

He twisted his head and managed to catch sight of her through a gap between two soldiers. Even more warm blood seeped over his chest, and he could not help thinking it was because the sight of her made his heart beat faster.

With a cry, Grace wrenched herself from Dahlia's arms and rushed out of the room.

She took all of the light with her. Black edged in on Jayden's vision, and despair filled his lungs, robbing him of breath. He could not blame her for leaving. He had attacked her. Become her very worst nightmare.

His vision began to fade and he heard an odd rattling sound that he realized was his attempt to breathe. He closed his eyes and hoped it would come quicker.

"Get the *fuck* out of my way!"

Jayden struggled to get his eyes open as shuffling erupted all around him. It took a moment for Jayden to focus, but when he did, he discovered Grace kneeling by his side, a determined look on her face.

She came back. Joy surged. Jayden focused all of his energy and managed to raise his hand. To touch her cheek.

His fingers left a smear of red upon her skin, and he dropped his hand in horror, never wanting to see blood upon her. "Proud of…you," he managed to whisper through clattering teeth. *So cold*. His lids grew too heavy. His head sank to the side.

The smell of peaches perfumed the air. A trickle on his chest. Warmth flooding him.

Breath shot into Jayden's lungs, and his eyes popped open. Inches from his face was Grace's hand. It cradled a pulverized piece of fruit.

Jayden slowly raised his eyes to hers. They were laden with hope. *Love*.

Thunder boomed, and Jayden's body contorted in agony as he screamed with all of his strength.

Chapter Eighteen

They all fell to their knees and clapped their hands over their ears as otherworldly thunder rolled throughout the room.

Grace wedged her head against her shoulder, trying to cover her ear that way so she could grope the air in front of her with one hand. She needed to find Jayden, to touch him, but her eyes wouldn't allow her to pry them open so she could see him.

A blast of energy exploded right in front of her, throwing her back several feet. She landed in a pile of twisted arms and legs belonging to the others in the room.

The blast of energy had come from where she'd last seen Jayden.

Now, she was able to force her eyes open. Her sight traveled the distance between her and the angel.

He writhed on the floor in a pool of his own blood. His hands, fingers spread painfully wide, slid through the slick redness, trying in vain to find purchase of some kind. His back was arched, his head thrown back. His mouth was wide open, and his desperate scream rent a hole straight through Grace.

Terror spiked, and Grace forced herself to move, crawling on her knees to where Jayden twisted on the floor. "No!" she shouted, the noise lost in the thunder and his scream.

This wasn't supposed to happen. She'd given him the fruit. It was supposed to heal him.

Her hands shoved the ripped and tattered fabric of his robe aside as he tossed and turned. Her hands sought out the wound.

It was…*gone*. He *had* healed. It just hadn't helped.

"Oh, God," Grace moaned, trying to embrace her angel. Had she caused this? She had to have. It was the only explanation.

Giving the fruit of the Tree of Eternal Life to the angel charged with ensuring it was never defiled? A sob barreled out of her chest. *Why would I do that?*

"I'm so sorry, angel." Her sobs distorted her words to the point where she knew he would never hear them, much less understand them over the pain that demanded so much more. She reached for him, trying to ease whatever anguish he was experiencing. She gathered him in her arms and pulled his head and shoulders into her lap.

He buried his face in her stomach and continued to scream, his body shaking with the pain that wracked him. His left hand grabbed her, digging into her back as he pushed his body as deeply as it would go into her lap. All the while, his screams and that thunder rent the air.

"Jayden, Jayden," she tried to coo through her hysteria. "I'm here. Shhh…"

She rocked him back and forth, her tears soaking his hair.

Then, suddenly, the thunder vanished. Jayden's scream cut off. The world fell into a deadly quiet.

Around the room, men and women slowly stood from wherever they had landed after the blast. They looked at one another in the silent, speculating shock that always followed natural disaster.

Grace only had eyes for the angel pressed against her stomach. Tremors shook his entire body, and his gasps and ragged breaths heated her skin.

He was still alive.

Tears still blurred her vision, but Grace forced her hand to move. Her trembling fingers sifted through his hair, gently pushing it away from his face. She needed to see him, to make sure he was still okay.

The angel took one last shuddering breath and slowly pulled back from her middle. He turned his face toward hers. His eyes remained clamped shut.

Unease lurched within her. Grace quickly scanned his body. He still had his wings. They were partially open and gleamed a very ordinary white. They'd lost the pearlescent sheen. Next to them, a soldier picked up a sword, and Grace realized with shock that it was *Jayden's* sword. The flames were gone.

She moaned. "What have I done to you?" She could never make this right. *Never.* Her fingers sank into his hair as she bowed her head and tried desperately not to break down completely.

His head moved beneath her hand. Her eyes sprang open to find him turning his face into her palm to press a kiss against her skin.

Grace gasped.

His eyelids fluttered open.

His eyes. That honey green color she loved…the honey was *gone.* He blinked once. Twice. A deep green stare looked up at her.

• • •

Such bliss.

The warmth of her skin. The scent of her. Her arms around him. Her fingers in his hair. The gray, stormy eyes he would spend the rest of his existence losing himself in.

The One. She is yours.

Jayden allowed his eyes to close briefly. *Oh, I know.* Absolute rightness settled down through his body, and his arms tightened around Grace's middle.

She stiffened within his hold and took a ragged breath. "Angel?" she asked tentatively.

He opened his eyes again and looked up into the face of the woman he loved. For the first time, he noticed the tear tracks down her cheeks, the dark hue in her eyes.

He frowned. "Grace?"

Her face crumbled before his eyes. Sobs burst from her so hard, her body lurched with them.

"Grace!" Jayden shifted as quickly as possible. Sitting up and reversing their positions, he pulled his woman into his lap.

She pressed her face against his throat; her tears coursed down his neck. "A-are you s-still an angel?"

Understanding.

She wept for him. For what she supposed he *lost*.

He had not thought it possible to love her more. With a finger beneath her chin, he directed her to look at him. The devastation in her eyes hurt him so badly he vowed he would never see such a thing in their gray depths again.

"*Are you?*" she whispered desperately.

He shook his head gently. "I am Fallen."

He felt the dread course through Grace, and he sent up a silent prayer of thanks that he had not lost the ability to read her thoughts. He loved his Grace's mind.

Before her dread could fully blossom, Jayden cupped her cheek and pressed a chaste kiss against her lips. "And I am so glad I am," he whispered.

He could sense her doubt, but before he could say anything to assuage it, a litany of words spilled from her lips.

"I am so sorry—if I knew the fruit would—how can you even *touch* me—I am so sorry. *So sorry.*"

His chuckle startled her to silence. She pulled back further to stare at him with a mixture of disbelief and insulted female pride.

Jayden's grin widened. "Grace, I was going to Fall anyway, love." Treasured memories of sleeping within her arms flooded him with warmth. *Oh, yes.* He had been at the perch of his Fall.

She sucked in a breath. "What?"

He trailed a finger down her adorable upturned nose and its smattering of freckles. "I could not be with you and remain an angel. I had already chosen you. It was only a matter of timing. And now it is out of the way. We can begin our lives together." As her relief reached him, his smile widened even more.

And then, Grace burst into loud sobs.

Jayden tightened his arms. "Grace!" He noticed they had an audience and quickly snapped his wings around them. "Grace, speak to me." She was relieved, and yet she cried. What was he to do to make it better?

She looked up at him through watery eyes. "I l-love you," she hiccupped.

"And that makes you *weep*?" he asked in horror.

Her sobs grew louder.

A burst of masculine laughter sounded over Jayden's left shoulder, and he turned his head to find Eli and Jericho looking upon them with mirth. Jericho clapped a hand on Jayden's shoulder. "Welcome to our world, man," the blond giant said. "Welcome to our world."

Eli chuckled. "Women do that. It's okay."

Jayden felt his body clench. "You can see us?" He rippled his wings to ensure himself that he had, indeed, enclosed Grace within them. And yet, the two men looked upon him and spoke to him.

The two men stopped laughing, and Jayden knew the look upon his face was grave, for his heart was so heavy he nearly joined his woman in her tears.

I can no longer make her disappear.

Of all of the things he could have lost in his Fall—

Her greatest wish, and I have failed her.

He felt her cool fingers on his cheek, closed his eyes, and braced himself for what he must tell her.

But when he turned his eyes upon her, she was gifting him with a wobbly smile. Jayden's words stalled in his throat as she trailed her fingertips across his lips.

"I'm going to tell Abi and Dahlia on you two," she said to Jericho and Eli while not taking her eyes from Jayden's. "'*Women do that.*" She snorted. "They'll kick your hineys."

Jayden stared mutely at her as her eyes brightened and her tears dried. He quickly scanned her thoughts. She *knew* his wings no longer hid her. She did not care.

I do not take what you need.

The deep resonant Voice rippled through Jayden's mind, causing him to gasp.

Jayden tentatively sent out a return thought: *Most High?*

I am here, son.

Now tears choked *Jayden's* throat. He snatched Grace even tighter, burying his face in the place between her neck and shoulder as emotion shuddered through him.

And with the love of the Most High echoing in his head, and the love of his woman warming his heart, Jayden knew that allowing himself to love had been the least weak thing he had ever done.

Epilogue

One Month Later

Jayden stared at the beginnings of spring out of the window of his office—he could still not believe he had one. The humans had quickly embraced him as one of their own, a demonstration of the love and charity he did not deserve, but vastly appreciated.

His office was right next door to Eli's. They had not given him a job description, really. He assumed he was the equivalent to "hired muscle." But this day, he might begin to earn his keep.

An uneasy feeling settled into Jayden's chest. Something in Heaven had shifted. While he had lost the invisibility of his wings, the rest of his powers had remained, and with it, an undeniable connection to the heavenly realm.

Something had happened. Someone had been given Jayden's job. He was sure of it. And if he could sense him or her, he could warn the others and help them prepare.

The Most High spoke to him: *Their mission does not come from me. An innocent is being used as a pawn.*

Through the happiness communion with the Most High always brought, Jayden nevertheless felt a pang of worry. He knew who the innocent was.

Anahita.

She was not headed toward them, however. Thankfulness that Jayden would not have to fight a dear friend filtered through him.

Jayden turned toward the door, ready to stride into Eli's office and share the news, but he stopped in his tracks.

His wife stood at the door. She was wearing that soft expression—a tantalizing mix of love and lust—that she always wore when she had been looking at him without his knowledge.

His heart lurched in his chest. Oh, how he loved this woman. "Wife," he whispered, beckoning her forward.

She came willingly into his arms and immediately raised her face for a kiss. He was more than happy to oblige. The kiss quickly launched out of control, as their kisses always did, and Jayden had to pull away to catch his breath. "What shall it be this time, love," he asked her with a smile. "Hard or soft?"

She tapped her chin for a moment and then answered with a sparkle in her eye, "How about hard, *then* soft?"

Jayden growled and swept her up into his arms, rushing off to their quarters. He could tell Eli about Anahita in an hour. Or two.

About the Author

When she's not writing or teaching, Micah Persell spends time with her husband and menagerie of pets in her Southern California home. *Of Consuming Fire* is her fourth novel; she has also published *Of Eternal Life* (Operation: Middle of the Garden #1), *Of the Knowledge of Good and Evil* (Operation: Middle of the Garden #2), and *Emma: The Wild and Wanton Edition*. Learn more about her at *www.micahpersell.com*, or visit her on *Facebook*, *Twitter*, and *Pinterest*.

More from This Author
(From *Of the Knowledge of Good and Evil*)

In her dreams, Dahlia was a free-range, castigating bitch. In real life?

Dahlia was an imprisoned, castigating bitch.

She sat with her back against the headboard. She rested her wrists on her bent knees and examined her nails with a critical eye. Beyond her nails, Dahlia caught a glimpse of her cell wall, and her relaxed lips quickly morphed into a grimace.

Three months she'd been a prisoner in this damn facility. Three months of being poked and prodded daily. And for what? A failed experiment that proved to turn her into some cosmic judge of character. Which was a freaking laugh riot, considering she was completely devoid of character herself.

But she wasn't in federal prison, and she had to remind herself often that all of this—testing both fruits; having to touch people over and over to determine if they were *good* or *evil*, an ability they'd termed the "Knowledge"; having to listen to their incessant talk of how the Knowledge would change espionage; being stuck in this terrible room—was worth it. They were lax on security here at the facility, and Dahlia never knew what life was going to throw at her, or when she was going to need to bail.

But—hand to God—she was going to kill someone if they forced her to touch and fruit-test one more do-good freak.

She heard a clatter at her cell door. Her head snapped up, and she watched through narrowed eyes as the door swung open and a man she hadn't seen before entered her cell.

Dahlia threw her head back and groaned to the ceiling. "God damn it. A new one?" She lowered her head and pinned him with a leer that had him squirming where he stood. "Is this really necessary, or are you just here so I'll touch you?"

Eli Johnson, bane of her existence and co-director of Operation: Middle of the Garden, entered the room behind the man who now looked like he faced a firing squad instead of one curvy Latina in a cell. "Knock it off, Dahlia," Eli said with a growl as he walked around his cohort. "He's not here for tests. He's here for—" He broke off to plow his fingers through his hair, and Dahlia silently congratulated herself for managing to stress him out with minimal effort. He was usually more unflappable than this. Today was looking up.

Eli took a deep breath, and then, "How are you finding your accommodations?"

For the first time in a long time, Dahlia grew wary. "Um… why?" she asked.

Eli shrugged. "We've been re-evaluating the conditions of your imprisonment. It's been suggested that you may enjoy visitation. Perhaps from friends. Or family."

Black ice filled her veins. "I don't have family."

They both looked at her for way longer than was comfortable, but Dahlia schooled her features into a mask. They could look all damn day. The answer wouldn't change. Not for them. Not for anyone.

"Okay," Eli said. "Just thought I'd ask." He then held his hand out, and the other man slapped an envelope into the open palm and then made a notation on the clipboard he carried. Eli strode forward and stopped right beside her bed. Dahlia realized she was holding her breath. "We had your mail forwarded here," he said.

Dahlia straightened.

"This came for you today." Eli dropped the envelope onto Dahlia's bed.

With measured slowness, Dahlia picked up the envelope, saw there was no return address, and turned it over. She cursed. "It's been opened," she accused. Rage flooded her.

Eli shrugged. "You're a prisoner."

As Dahlia saw red, Eli and the stranger left the cell. When the door clicked behind them, Dahlia tore the letter from the envelope. One flick of her wrist, and it was open. The world tilted violently.

Ha pasado.

It's happened. The Spanish words blurred before her eyes as the letter fell to the floor. Blood drained from her face. She tried to pull air into her lungs, but her body wasn't cooperating.

Not this. Anything but this. Everything she'd done, all the people she'd hurt. Killed. She'd done everything to avoid this exact letter.

At the edge of hysteria, Dahlia managed to pull herself back. In the back of her mind, she'd always known this day would come. She would handle it. She would—

Her eyes flew to the door.

This was the reason she was here. Here and not in federal prison. Her eyes evaluated the riveted steel that separated her from the "good" folks. She strode to the door and kicked it with all her might. At the sight of her boot's imprint in the titanium steel, a grim smile spread her cheeks.

She drew back for another kick.

• • •

In his dreams, his Emily was alive. In real life?

Jericho was alone. Tormented by her memory.

The worst part was when he woke up, and for a few blissful moments, he didn't remember she was dead. He would roll over and reach for her, ready to pull her warm body into his own, and his hand would grasp air.

Just like it was doing right now.

The weight of his loss settled in on his heart, and Jericho squeezed his eyes shut tighter, prolonging the visual confirmation of Emily's absence a few moments longer. But the delay only caused horrific scenes to flicker against the black of his closed eyelids. The longing to sift his fingers through Emily's shoulder-length brown hair, to gaze into her large, expressive honey-colored eyes shifted as images of her sweat-soaked hair, screams of terror, and vacant eyes crowded happy memories to the back of his mind.

Jericho shook. The fruit forced his remembrances to maintain their perfect sensory detail. He could never forget her; his memories would never begin to fade.

And after eight years, he was ashamed to admit he wanted them to. He'd loved Emily with every fiber of his soul. He'd lived for her. He still lived for her, even though he'd been with Emily for only a handful of days.

He spent his time in equal parts grief, equal parts resentment that he couldn't shake the hold his mate had over him after the unfairly short amount of time they'd had together. If anyone had told him he'd spend eight years grieving his mate of only five days, he might have run screaming at his first sight of her.

Might have. Oh, who was he kidding. Nothing could have kept him from Emily. Nothing but death. A death he'd caused.

He'd give anything to set that guilt aside.

A resounding boom ricocheted through Jericho's room, pulling him from his thoughts. The picture frames on the wall shuddered and clacked. Jericho frowned and pulled himself to a sitting position, wondering if the noise had been dream or reality.

The boom sounded again, followed by a crash. Jericho's sleepy confusion evaporated. Something was happening. Apprehension settled into his gut.

Jericho walked to the door. Shouts bounced in the hallway, and for the first time since entering this room months ago, Jericho placed his hand on the doorknob. He took a deep breath and steeled himself to leave the solace of his room. He turned his wrist. The knob didn't budge.

Jericho frowned. His door was never locked. Granted, he hadn't tried it in all this time, but he had always known he was free to come and go as he pleased. He just didn't please.

The back of his neck tingled, and Jericho froze. The metal of the doorknob seemed to burn his hand. He brought his eyes up to the window of his door, and what he saw stole the breath from his lungs.

Eyes as dark as espresso. Smooth, luminous brown skin. Cascades of wavy, rich black hair. As he felt his own eyes widen in shock, hers did as well.

The One. She's yours.

The words stopped his heart. They were the same words he'd heard a mysterious Voice whisper eight years ago when he'd first laid eyes on Emily.

His body moved on its own to press against the door. The tips of his fingers skimmed over the cool metal on their way to the window, and his hand splayed on the glass.

Those beautiful eyes zeroed in on his hand, and her lips parted. Her brows drew together as she watched her own hand rise to meet his on the other side of the glass. His hand dwarfed hers—he couldn't even see it past his own fingers and wide palm—but he swore he could feel the heat of her skin through the barrier.

No, no, no. This couldn't be happening. He'd found—and lost—his mate. He didn't get another.

God, did he?

The weight of gloom lifted from his shoulders. Hope bubbled up through his chest, and he felt an unfamiliar pull at his cheeks. A quick check of his reflection in the glass showed he was smiling.

His heart started beating again in double time. He moved to try the doorknob once more, but before he could, he felt it turning against his palm and realized that he hadn't been able to open the door because she had been holding the knob in her grip. And now, she was coming in to him. His grin grew broader, and he refocused on her gorgeous features.

She stopped twisting the knob. Her dazed eyes grew sharp, and she jerked her palm from the window where it rested against his.

Jericho's grin slid from his face.

She bared her teeth at him and with a vicious twist of her shoulders, the door screeched. She stepped back and held the mangled doorknob before her.

Jericho looked down to where his hand rested on his side of the knob and gave it a twist. It didn't budge. His eyes flew back to the window, and he couldn't prevent them from raking over her form. She was perfection. Tall. Curvaceous. Seductive. The hand he pressed against the window curled into a fist.

She sneered at him, dropping the knob from the tips of her fingers. He could hear the clunk as it hit the floor.

And then, with one final look of disgust, she turned her back on him and ran away.

In the mood for more Crimson Romance?
Check out *Fusion*
by Candace Sams
at *CrimsonRomance.com*.